# Death Takes Me

# Death Takes Me

*Cristina Rivera Garza*

*A Novel*

TRANSLATED BY SARAH BOOKER
AND ROBIN MYERS

HOGARTH
*New York*

. . . victims of the questions: Who is killing me? To whom am I giving myself over to be killed?

—HÉLÈNE CIXOUS

# I

## The Castrated Men

However, with humans, castration should not be understood as the basis for denying the possibility of the sexual relation, but as the prerequisite for any sexual relation at all. It can even be said that it is only because subjects are castrated that human relations as such can exist. Castration enables the subject to take others as Other rather than the same, since it is only after undergoing symbolic castration that the subject becomes preoccupied with questions such as "what does the Other want?" and "what am I for the Other?"

—RENATA SALECL

. . . victims of the questions: Who is killing me? To whom am I giving myself over to be killed?

—HÉLÈNE CIXOUS

# I

# The Castrated Men

However, with humans, castration should not be understood as the basis for denying the possibility of the sexual relation, but as the prerequisite for any sexual relation at all. It can even be said that it is only because subjects are castrated that human relations as such can exist. Castration enables the subject to take others as Other rather than the same, since it is only after undergoing symbolic castration that the subject becomes preoccupied with questions such as "what does the Other want?" and "what am I for the Other?"

—RENATA SALECL

# 1

## What I Believed I Said

"That's a body," I muttered to no one or to someone inside me or to nothing. I didn't recognize the words at first. I said something. And what I said or believed I said was for no one or for nothing or it was for me, listening to myself from afar, from that deep inner place the air or light never reaches; where the murmur began, hostile and greedy, the rushed, voiceless breath. A passageway. A forest. I said it after the alarm, after the disbelief. I said it when my eye was able to rest. After the long spell it took for me to give it form (something visible) (something utterable). I didn't say it: it came out of my mouth. The low voice. The tone of terror. Or of intimacy.

"Yes, it's a body," I had to say, and instantly closed my eyes. Then, almost immediately, I opened them again. I had to say it. I don't know why. What for. But I looked up and, since I was exposed, I fell. Seldom the knees. My knees yielded to the weight of my body, and the vapor of my faltering breath clouded my vision. Trembling. Leaves tremble, and bodies. Seldom the thundering of bones. Crick. On the pavement, to one side of the pool of blood, there. Crack. His folded legs, his insteps face-up, the palms of his hands. The pavement is made up of tiny rocks.

"It's a body," I said or had to say, barely stammered, to no one or to me, who could not believe it, who refused to believe me, who never believed. Eyes open, disproportionately. The wail. Seldom the wail. That invocation. That crude prayer. I was studying it. There was no way out or cure for it. There was nothing inside and, around me, there was just a body. What I believed I said. A collection of impossible angles. A skin, the skin. Something on the asphalt. Knee. Shoulder. Nose. Something broken. Something dislocated. Ear. Foot. Sex. An open, red thing. A context. A boiling point. Something undone.

"A body," I believed I said or barely muttered for no one or for me who was becoming a forest or passageway, an entrance orifice. Blackness. I believed I said. Seldom the lips that refuse to close. The shame. His final minute. His final image. His final complete sentence. The nostalgia for it all. Seldom. Staying still.

When I said again what I believed I said, when I said it to myself, the only person listening to me from that far-off inner place where air and light are generated and consumed, it was already too late: I had made the necessary calls, and because I was the one who had found him, I had already become the Informant.

# 2

## My First Body

*No, I didn't know him.*

*No, I've never seen anything like it.*

*No.*

It's difficult to explain what you do. It's difficult to tell someone as they interrogate you with a brown, vehement, crepuscular gaze that it's better, or at least more interesting, to run through alleys than on the city streets. Is a city a cemetery? That it's even better to run there than on a track. A blue place. Something that isn't a lake. The knees are the problem, clearly. And the danger. It's difficult to confess to an official from the Department of Homicide Investigation that danger is, precisely, the allure. That the allure is the unexpected. Something different. It is difficult to detail, in all its slow dispersion, your daily routine, so that someone interested in something else, someone interested in solving a crime, will understand that running through the alleys of the city is a better alternative to running on tracks or on illuminated sidewalks: that is a difficult thing. To tell her: that's really it, officer, the danger: what's hiding there: what doesn't happen elsewhere. It's difficult to speak in monosyllables.

*I was running. I usually run at dusk. Also at dawn, but usually at dusk. I run on the track. I run from the coffee shop to my apart-*

*ment. I avoid sidewalks and roads; I prefer shortcuts. Alleys. Narrow streets. No, I don't run for exercise. I run for pleasure. To get somewhere. I run, if you will, utilitarianly.*

There's no time to say it. It wouldn't interest her. But running, this is what I think, is a mental thing. In every runner there should be a mind that runs. The goal is pleasure. The mind's challenge consists of staying in place: of the breathing, of the panting, of the knee, of the hand, of the sweat. If it goes elsewhere, it loses. If it wanders off, it loses even more. The mind's challenge is to be the body. If it aspires to it, if it achieves it, the mind then becomes the accomplice, and there, from that complicity, the detour that moves the mind and body away from boredom emerges. The detour is the pleasure. The goal.

*Yes, sometimes there are dead cats. Pigeons. No, never men. Never women. No, none of that. This is my first body.*

It's difficult to speak to you informally. Why would that be?

To see you: well-groomed, white shirt, patent leather shoes. We know that everything is a cemetery. An apparition is always an apparition. You tell me nothing changes. Why shouldn't that be questioned? I'm sure you know how to whistle. You have that kind of mouth over the half-open mouth that neither air nor night comes through. My first.

*Sometimes junkies. They share needles. They offer them. Yes. No. I just run. That's all.*

*The endorphins, they explain to me, cause addiction. You start to run and then you can't stop. If that counts, then yes. Addict.*

First there's the sensation of reality that prompts the falling onto your own two feet. Once. Again. Once and again. Measured, the trot. The steps. It's possible that someone runs away, frenzied. That intermittent relationship between the ground and the body—the weight of the two. Gravity and anti-gravity. A dialogue. A burning discussion. And the relationship, also intermittent, between the landscape and the mind. The silhouettes of the trees and the flow of the blood. Everything happens so quickly at the end, that's what they say. The colors of the cars and the more recent concern. The angles of the windows and the memory or the pain. An entire life: the words: an entire life. The struggle, always ferocious, to concentrate. I am here. I am now. That's called I Am My Breath. The internal sound. The rhythm. The weight. The scandalous murmur of the *I* within the dark fishbowl of the skeleton. But it's still so difficult to speak to you informally. Only later the loud noise. The ardor. The air that seems to thin out in the nasal cavities: narrow ridges in the lungs. An implosion. That violent unleashing of the endorphins, producing a euphoria that in many ways resembles desire or love or pleasure. What will come of all this, my First? The lightness. The speed. The possibility of levitating. When I start running, that's the moment I'm searching for. That's the moment I pursue. That's the goal.

*Yes, I write. Also. Also for pleasure, like running. To get somewhere. Utilitarianly. To get to the end of the page, I mean. Not for exercise. If you know what I mean: it's life or death.*

It's difficult to explain what you do. The reasons. The consequences. The processes. It's difficult to explain what you do without uncontrollably bursting into laughter or tears. My eye is looking at me now, unguarded. Before the image of the murdered body that inserts itself like white noise into the interrogation; before what we no longer see but can't stop seeing, what the hell does it matter if we get to the end of the page or not? It's a rectangle, don't you see? I ask her. I'm not in any shape to say that doing this, getting to the end of the page, is a matter of life, a matter of death. Where's the blood to prove it? you ask me. Where's my blood? You nod, perplexed.

*No, I'd never seen him in the neighborhood.*

*Yes, I do generally pay attention to those things. New faces.*

*Lost pets. Businesses. Yes, personal, social interactions. But I hadn't seen him around here. No.*

*I'm sure.*

*Yes, I'm aware that he was missing a penis. Mutilation. Theft. The lack. I'm aware of all this.*

*Yes, it's a terrible thing against the dead.*

*I can't anymore.*

*I'm sure.*

*A terrible thing. Yes. Against the dead.*

# 3

## The Poetry Field of Action

The Detective from the Department of Homicide Investigation showed me a photograph of the bricks in the wall outside the Chinese restaurant, specifically the bricks from the corner where the restaurant ends and behind which the Alley of the Castrated Man unfolds with its monumental narrowness. They were already calling it that. It was almost immediate. The bricks, I couldn't help but notice, were covered with the unreal light that often gets me out of the house and demands I inhale the air of the world at 6:15 in the evening. All this in the city.

"Do you recognize this?" the official asked with her gaze on the bridge of my nose, the tips of my eyelashes. Without taking my eyes off the box, I fell silent. I looked. I examined.

They weren't hard to find. These diminutive words, painted with coral-colored nail polish, were there, on that corner, under that hypothetical light, over the uneven texture of a brick:

> beware of me, my love
> beware of the silent woman in the desert
> of the traveler with an emptied glass
> and of her shadow's shadow

"Quite literary, don't you think?" the Detective insisted into my silence. "Your field of action, am I right?"

I smiled at her because I had never thought of poetry as a "field of action," and because Alejandra Pizarnik's lines were indeed present in a sudden here and now, a great, terrible thing against the dead. A deed. Rage in diminutive letters. Something tiny.

I didn't look at her. I avoided looking at her. I kept staring at the photograph. I saw something else instead, you always see something else. I saw the images of an installation: *Great Deeds Against the Dead,* 1994. Fiberglass, resin, paint, artificial hair, 277 x 244 x 152 centimeters. Jake and Dinos Chapman, born in the sixties, had arranged three life-size male figures around a tree trunk. Tied and naked, arranged in positions with vaguely religious resonances (a crucified body, open arms), the men hanging from the trunks were missing their genitals. I saw that. There, where a penis and testicles should have been, in their place, was tarnished, earthly flesh. Absence in red. Castration. All of it enveloped in the acrid stench of blood. All that in London. Jake and Dinos Chapman had declared to the press that they conceptualized themselves as a pair of sore-eyed scopophiliac oxymorons. Jake and Dinos Chapman claimed they were artists. I saw something else, and as a result, I saw you. A city is always a cemetery.

We were in the Detective's office—a basement quivering with the sound of uneven voices and the blank velocity of papers passed from hand to hand—and, perhaps because of that, the minuscule words in nail polish seemed both more threatening and funnier. A children's story. That type of cruelty. In this place where it felt like no light but the artificial kind could reach, where the Detective's eyes surely got used to their own opacity, the words of Alejandra Pizarnik made it so that the world out there, the world that had killed her, seemed benign or banal.

"They're brutal words," I finally said, looking her in the eye, accepting her challenge. *"The traveler with an emptied glass,"* I repeated as if I were reciting it before a hushed crowd made up entirely of children, *"of her shadow's shadow,"* I enunciated, slowly, as I realized that the Detective's dark brown eyes, insistently watching me, full of concentration, the type of concentration that has always made me think of a mind while writing, were lit up. "Pizarnik always did that very well. Wrote brutal things."

The Detective smiled at me. An echo. Something distant.

"I knew it," she said, a strange inflection in some part of her voice as her hand leapt to my right elbow, lightly guiding my body, gracefully even, out of her basement. "I knew you and I would talk a lot about poetry."

It wasn't until after, long after, that I understood: the last thing she said was not an invitation but a threat.

I reached the door to my apartment; as I turned the key for the third time to the left, I wondered if she'd been there, too. The installation hadn't been in the city all that long ago, and I'm sure this is why the phrase I'd uttered in the Detective's basement, probably at random, evoked the memory: *Great Deeds Against the Dead.* An incomplete, biased, real translation. An echo of Goya. A reverberation of the war. Great things, yes, terrible things against the dead. That touch us. Deeds against them. *Beware of me, my love.* I wondered if the Detective had also seen it or if she had only been referencing the engraving. The original. Francisco de Goya y Lucientes: *Sad forebodings of what is going to happen. Bury them and keep quiet. There is no time left. Even worse. This is too much. This is worse. Great Deeds! With dead men! I saw it. This is bad. The worst is to beg. What is the use of a cup? The results. Truth has died. This is how it happened.*

I wondered if maybe she hadn't seen anything. If it had been nothing but a great coincidence.

As the door slowly gave way to the key's clumsy buffeting, I
remembered that Goya had said all that on a metal sheet. The titles like scraps of dialogue among the dead. The pencil wet with
special ink on a plate protected with powdered resin. Then the
heat, and the resin just adhered to the metal, producing a granular
surface. All this in a city named Madrid. The wake of the resis-
tance against the invasion of a man named Bonaparte. An upris-
ing: eighty-five metal sheets, forty-five on the massacre and sixteen
on the famine that, a couple years later, caused twenty thousand
deaths, his wife's among them. *Fatal consequences of the war.*
That's what Goya said. The metal plate coated with varnish and
then, within the acid, only within the acid, the grooves marked in
copper. The lesion emerged. The fingers of my imagination
touched it, that lesion, in the static air of the apartment, when I
was finally inside. The illuminated lesion. My eyes fell on it once
and again. The cut. The fissure. Obsessive, my eyes. Incapable of
seeing anything else. I fell onto the couch. Seldom the knees. My
bag on the ground. The air that finally escaped through my mouth.
I don't know how to whistle. I remembered that. Then I wondered, there, immobile, curled up on the soft surface of the sofa
(my left cheek on the seat) (my right hand hanging, orphaned, almost touching the floor), if the Detective, who surely had been
there, at the much-talked-about exhibition of the Chapman brothers, would have held, with a delicacy I found difficult to picture,
the tall glass of champagne as she strolled around, with the tired
tone of someone who has already seen it all, with that smug or
prudent indifference, how incredible, how shockingly incredible
it always was to see, regardless whether it was Goya or the Chapman brothers, an etching or an installation or a real event, the
body of a castrated man. I wondered, still curled up there, my
knees almost at my mouth, my right hand now brushing the floor,

if the Detective, who had just barely finished interrogating me with great meticulousness and without any sign of tiring, with a discipline so fierce that it seemed not particularly human, had enjoyed the cocktail. The bubbles of the champagne. The light vaporous seething inebriation. The murmurs.

# 4

## *Victim* Is Always Feminine

It was after the third murder that the Detective sought me out again. She called me, and we arranged to meet in the café next to the Chinese restaurant. When I arrived, still panting after my fifteen-minute sprint, she was already waiting for me with an Americano—no sugar—on the empty side of the table. Her fingers drumming the beat of an old melody. The instantaneous impression that the woman lived inside a house with green walls was immediately followed by the impression that the woman didn't have a house. No walls around her.

"So you're still running," she commented with that strange accent in some corner of her voice, in its outskirts, almost. In response, I nodded and moved toward the bar to say hello to the owner and ask for a glass of water.

Someone runs, I told you, convinced that everything was a cemetery. Later I acted as if nothing were happening. As if you weren't happening.

"Am I interrupting your work?" she asked as she swiveled her seat around. It was clear she was no expert in the field of insipid small talk and was impatient to get to the point and address the matter that had brought us there, face-to-face in a frank attitude of expectation.

"My work is a continuous interruption," I answered drolly, irresponsibly, trying to avoid the topic because I found myself—but the Detective had no way of knowing this—in one of those silent, unproductive cycles that, on other occasions, mostly before I picked up running, had sent me out to directly observe, in an obsessive immobility, the sky.

"I suppose you're already aware," she whispered and bent over her cup of coffee just to have the opportunity to look up from there. An abyss in her movement.

"It's been in all the papers," I confirmed.

"An interesting case, don't you think?"

I thought—and here to think really means to produce an image—about the castrated bodies of the three young men who had appeared, naked and bloody, on the city's asphalt. I thought—and here to think really means to hear the echo—about the word castration and all the tragic references of the term. I thought—and here to think really means to see—about how long, about how interminable, about how incessant the word dis-mem-ber-ment was. I thought—and here to think means to quietly pronounce—about the term serial murders and I realized it was the first time I connected it with the male body. And I thought—and here to think really means to practice irony—that it was interesting in and of itself how, at least in Spanish, the word victim, or víctima, is always feminine.

"Are you laughing?" the Detective interrupted. Intrigued. Annoyed.

And it was right then that I thought, in the most untimely way, just like those clear days that appear amid the ashen ones preceding the explosion of springtime, that the murderer was really a murderess.

And then I saw you out of the corner of my eye, like someone waiting to reach a difficult agreement. Like someone hopelessly waiting in a train station; like someone. The train passing by. The hand, shaken.

"It's the word víctima, Detective," I explained without any hope of being understood as I wrote the definite article and the noun on a paper napkin. "*La* víctima is always feminine. Do you see? In the recounting of the facts, in the newspaper articles, in the essays that will be written about these events, this word will castrate them over and over again."

Over and over again. The echo. Over. Over again. The repetition. The sonorous phenomenon occurred, we both realized, when the café owner softly sang *Gee baby, ain't I good to you,* and the coincidence, the dark humor of the coincidence, provoked a burst of laughter that I couldn't repress.

"And you find that funny?"

"The song on the radio?" I asked, trying unsuccessfully to draw her attention to what had just happened on the threshold of her ears. It can take so much work to listen to a song. I thought that. I thought: it takes so much effort to believe what's right before your eyes. And then, out of pure pleasure, I winked at you.

"The castration. The double castration," the Detective clarified, concentrating on her objective and oblivious to everything else.

"No," I told her after giving it some thought. "No, I don't find it funny at all."

I'm sure I was telling the truth.

Then, without any transition, as if the Detective were rigorously following a screenplay I hadn't read but was participating in, she said, "This was found in the hand of the second body," and placed on the table a white sheet of paper within which or on which someone had arranged a series of letters clipped from newspapers or magazines, making them, then, in the act itself, castrated letters, and simultaneously establishing not the absence but what was absent within the sheet. It was, of course, another Alejandra Pizarnik poem:

NOW THEN: Who will stop plunging their hands in search of tributes for the forgotten girl? The cold will pay. The wind will pay. As will the rain. And the thunder. *For Aurora and Julio Cortázar.*

I looked at it again, slowly, unable to believe that a woman so professional in appearance had just placed a sheet of paper that was a piece of evidence in my hands. The original. I ran my fingertips over its surface. I brought it close to my nose, expecting a peculiar aroma. The tribute. The plunging hands.

"*Diana's Tree,*" I murmured without thinking about it, without really knowing how it was that I knew it or why I remembered it so clearly. "From 1962."

"You know it?" the Detective immediately asked, and I couldn't help but note she hadn't called it a "poem" or a "line."

"Everyone knows it," I told her, heedless of the arrogance. "Everyone in the poetry field of action," I corrected myself. And before looking at the photograph in which the third Pizarnikian message appeared, I also couldn't help but see that on the very surface of the name Cortázar there were hiding, threatening, a court and a tzar—words that, in that moment, lacked all innocence.

The third message, written in lipstick on the sidewalk, said:

she says she doesn't know the fear of death of love
she says she fears the death of love
she says love is death is fear

she says death is fear is love
she says she doesn't know

The photograph of a poem. That's what I had in my hands: the photograph of a poem. To realize that I had the photograph of a poem in my hands sparked a strange fury in me. Something like a shadow passed over the roof. That's what some call melancholia. Or tree. Isn't that true? Alejandra Pizarnik's words left you speechless for a long time, that's what I perceived.

"Tell me, please, Cristina, who is the 'everyone' who knows this kind of poetry so well?" And then I looked at the Detective again as if I'd just come back from a long journey or woken up from a very dark dream. Poetry. *This kind of poetry.*

# 5

## The Suspectress

I mentioned it to my Lover while we were lying naked in bed. A Sunday. I told him I'd met with the Detective in charge of the Castrated Men case a few days back. When I said this, when I pronounced the words *castrated men* as if they were italicized, I'm sure I couldn't repress a scandalous little giggle, a possibly insipid sound with which I tried to downplay both the reality of the facts and my meeting with the Detective. I described her almost immediately. I told him she was a woman with opaque eyes and huge hands. I told him she had an office in a basement where nothing but artificial light ever shone. I told him, very close to his neck, my left arm resting almost weightlessly on his shoulder, that the Detective had shown me the Alejandra Pizarnik poems that had appeared close to or at the scene of the crime itself. Three little poems. Three tiny messages. Then I thought of you, certainly. Later I was pensive and unwittingly kept silent. I listened to the echo of the threat: *The wind will pay. As will the rain. And the thunder.* I saw my hand, slack against his torso, and I saw the hand, the other hand, a minuscule hand, plunged in a chasm of viscera. *The fear of death of love,* I heard that line like a whisper very close to my ear. A tribute. *She says she doesn't know.*

And then I saw you; I did it again. So difficult sometimes to believe that, seeing you. And yet so natural. Certainly you get used to everything. I was going to give you a name, but at the last minute, I pictured the shadow a willow casts. I don't know if it's possible to live like this, you said from afar. I didn't lie to you.

In the end, I didn't tell my Lover that the Detective walked too quickly: her long steps, a certain rigidity in her joints, her forward gaze. Nor did I mention the sort of accent that seeped, with great control, into the ends of her sentences. I avoided telling him that every time I met with her, I was overwhelmed by the strange sensation, the uncomfortable sensation, that I knew her from before. It wasn't, of course, due to the familiarity earned through continuous and profound negotiation—I would have remembered *that* immediately—but from the knowledge forged, sinuously, morosely, in the most futile coincidences. I sensed it happening the moment you winked at me. I was thinking about coincidences; meanwhile, you winked at me. For a ravaged mess in the middle of the street, you certainly had a great sense of humor. That relaxed me. That made me believe I could keep living. Invoking. This: perhaps that woman and I had attended a conference where both of us, from different corners of the facility, asked similar questions. Did you know that apple trees are an enigma, Professor? Is this really a castle? Perhaps we had taken the same airplane to cross the same ocean and waited afterward, next to each other, for the luggage circulating on the same belt. The Detective would have caught my attention in those circumstances. I didn't tell the Lover that, either, but I whispered it to you in a discreet aside. She was that kind of person: anodyne in appearance but full of gravitas; a presence both obvious and silent. Someone interesting. She tends to express herself like that.

Had our paths crossed in such a way, I would have looked at her cautiously, barely sliding my pupils around my eye socket to keep from moving, and I would certainly have invented a story for her.

I would have said: That opaque-eyed woman in the blue uniform is a teacher or a policewoman. She lives alone. She talks alone. She eats alone. I would have described her gaze as grave or intense or tragic. And then, in the story, I would have asked her to look at me. I would have laughed at myself, and with no better explanation, I would have picked up my suitcase and continued on my way. Suitcases tend to be heavy. They are so heavy. The Lover, who listened attentively to the silence in which I held everything I avoided saying without knowing why, turned over, wrapped his right arm around my left shoulder, and smiled with that open and luminous smile that was the reason he found himself under the sheets, on my bed, next to my body.

"So?" he said. "Are you a suspect?"

From those early days I remember the wind above all. The sound of the wind. It seeped through the cracks in the windows, under the door, through the pores of my body. It shook the poplar leaves and the telephone wires. The world found itself in the state of millimetric shock that is sometimes described with the adjective "tremulous." And, with the wind, the dust storm arrived. I remember all this. The dust storm and, beneath the dust storm, your appearance. Someone to address informally. Sometimes the dust storm intensified into giant vertical whirlwinds, but usually it was nothing but a curtain of subdued brown tones that obstructed the view. The murders began during those tremulous, ashen February days, but they only took place, like the first one did, on the few days of diaphanous clarity that interrupted, as if by magic, the ravages of the dust. Thus, when the light burst onto the backs of the poplar leaves, giving them the aura of something divine, under a scandalously blue sky, a man was dying. A man was waking up castrated.

# 6

## I and Who I Was

I've said it several times, both in public and in private: I do not lead an interesting life. Though many would say that my field of action, as the Detective called it, is fiction, I've always secretly believed that my field, my action, belongs to poetry. Although this is because I consider poetry, in the most traditional and hierarchical sense, to be the crown of all writing, the goal of all writing, I rarely admit it to myself, much less to others. To accept such a thing would provoke great shame and great sorrow in me. To avoid both sensations, I usually say that I'm a professor and that I like to run. If the questions continue, I may go on to admit that I write, but leave out the titles and number of books I've published. If pressed, I acknowledge that I like the peace of my office and the warmth of my apartment, especially the big bedroom windows that overlook the park where, with similar conviction, if in total chaos, the poplars and pine trees grow. In any case, whether or not I say so in ceding to questions from others, it would be quite reasonable to describe my life as stable. Other equally precise adjectives would be: comfortable, relaxed, routine, pleasant. It surprised me that the Lover with the Luminous Smile would believe, even for a fleeting instant, that I could be suspected of such cruel crimes, it's true, but I didn't mind. His light joke indicated to me that in some part of his head or desire he conceived of me or produced me as a woman that, being me, was really another person. A serial killer. Someone with sufficient cruelty or frustration or madness to attack men and violently, furiously, or indifferently cut off their genitals. Someone with sufficient physical force to drag the dismembered bodies down narrow alleys or along dark sidewalks. Someone, too, with sufficient delicacy to transcribe, with fingernail polish or lipstick, entire poems by Alejandra Pizarnik. Someone with abysses under their wrists. Someone with complicated eyes and tremulous hands. The hatred. The revenge. That the Lover with the Luminous Smile could consider me, again, even for the most fleeting of instants, even within the conspiratorial humor that precedes amorous sessions, a castrator, is something I found quite hilarious. So hilarious that I let out a long cackle and kissed him full on the mouth. So hilarious that I bit his nipples and pulled his thick mat of hair with a tenderness I only began to feel just then. It's truly strange, I told you, how tenderness sometimes crops up. But as you weren't there, you didn't hear. As if to guide his hand toward my pubis as I mounted his hips. To pronounce the words: "These are two bodies." Enough to sustain, a little while later, a meditative silence at the very moment when he closed his eyes and exhaled, with delight, with a grimace of pain, with something like delirium, the breath of his pleasure. This. The last one.

I can still see myself looking at him: a body within another, interwoven, exhausted. His sex engulfed by mine. Great deeds, yes. Two bodies.

I can still hear the howl of the wind. And I blink. Once. And again. The goose bumps from what I observe: the absence. The unprecedented castration. What cannot be observed. I still await the coming of blood. A drop. A flow. The dizziness. The weeping of the next of kin. The news of the death. The general stupefaction. I am still infuriated by the curious onlookers who lean out to see, to see you on the inside. To save themselves.

I'm still moved by the words that descended in droves, uninvited, and settled on the pillow:

> now
> at this innocent hour
> the one I used to be sits with me
> along my peripheral vision

# 7

## How to Read Poetry

When she asked, I told her the truth: I wasn't an expert on the subject. I had indeed read Alejandra Pizarnik—first because of the morbid curiosity inspired by the image of a suicidal poet; then because her books were difficult to find, making them expensive cult objects; and later, almost at the end, out of pleasure. That's what I said: out of pleasure. And then I added: out of terror. Because she uttered words that lodged in my throat. Because she made her vertiginous descent into musical, bloody infernos that frankly made me feel as much attraction as fear. Because she was playful.

The Detective looked at me suspiciously. She rose from the chair in front of my desk and began, without asking permission, to examine all the books on the shelves that almost covered the walls of the office. Her hand like a brush on the spines.

"Do you remember the second man's poem?" she asked. Before I had time to answer, she added, her back still to me: "The cold will pay. The wind will pay. As will the rain. And the thunder."

Her reasoning turned out to be obvious: There was a warning in these words, a sign she wanted to follow. A clue. I didn't laugh this time, but I did stand up.

"That isn't how you read poetry," I whispered, increasingly dumbfounded. "Poetry isn't denotative. It isn't like a manual," I was going to continue, but she interrupted me with a firm voice, and if I hadn't known she was an officer in service of the Department of Homicide Investigation, I still would have recognized it as the voice of an expert.

"But according to what I've read," she said, turning her face toward me in a dramatic arc, "it can be prophetic. At least that's what some poets believe. That it has the power of prophecy."

Defeated, I returned to my side of the desk and fell into the chair. If you'd been there, resting each of your palms on each of my shoulders, I would have been able to laugh. I would have been able to tell her: what I want is to stop seeing it. The noise of the wind seeped, as it had been doing for days, through the bottom crack of the window, and the sound automatically made me uneasy, an unnecessary internal turbulence. I wondered, though I wasn't prepared to think about this kind of thing, if another man might die right then. If that man might be bathed in blood right now. Before me. The Detective, meanwhile, pulled out the complete collection of poetry by Alejandra Pizarnik, edited by Ana Becciú and published by Editorial Lumen, and she proceeded to read the back cover aloud, as if she were alone in my office, or as if she were the owner of the book:

> Born in Buenos Aires in 1936, Alejandra Pizarnik published her first poems when she was just twenty years old. In the early 1960s, she spent several years living in Paris, where she developed friendships with André Pierre de Mandiargues, Octavio Paz, Julio Cortázar, and Rosa Chacel. Upon her return to Buenos Aires, she dedicated the rest of her life to writing. She died in Buenos Aires on September 25, 1972.

Without pausing, she continued with fragments from the back cover:

One of the most emblematic figures of Hispanic literature, controversial, polemical, who became a myth among adolescents in the eighties and nineties . . . deep intimacy and severe sensuality . . . intense insomnia and midday lucidity . . . her poems spread love and fear everywhere.

"The rain," she interrupted herself, not closing the book, as if she hadn't realized that a new idea had come into her head and that she was, in fact, interrupting herself. "The cold. The thunder. Don't you think the next murder will happen in the rainy season?"

I hope I looked at her with the unease and incredulity I felt. Surely it was those two moods or those two emotions that led me straight to the irony.

"Officer, do you even know when the rainy season in Buenos Aires is? I mean," I added, "after all, Alejandra was talking about the Southern Cone."

The Detective closed the book, took her jacket from the coat rack, and winked her left eye.

"Don't be so literal," she said, just before opening the door. "That isn't how you read poetry. But thanks for the tip."

And that's how, without even asking for permission, the Detective began to speak with me informally.

# 8

## All the Fields
## All the Battles

Obsessive, the eyes. Seeing nothing else. Never again the poplars or the wind or the sunrise. Never again the romp. Seldom the respiration. Everywhere the mark: furrows on sheets of copper; furrows on sheets of flesh. The acid that reveals. The memory. The image. Someone takes the puncturing object. Someone brandishes it: thing in the air. Reflection. Someone chooses or finds or produces the entrance orifice. Seldom the teeth. Someone scratches, opens, searches. Someone extracts the gonad, the testicle, the sexual organ. Does Someone smile? Does Someone follow the law? Does Someone grieve? Does Someone fill with blood or hatred? Does Someone execute a vengeance or a promise? Does Someone use gloves? On the pavement. In Byzantium. On the ships that cross the Atlantic. In an alleyway. On the hospital bed. In the Naples bedchambers. On the battlefield. All the fields. All the battles. In a basement. Someone punishes [Sima Qian (145–90 B.C.E.)] [Pierre Abélard (1079–1142)]. Someone approaches the boy who lies, sedate, in a bathtub of tepid milk. The smell of spices. Someone believes in the broadest tessitura [Carlo Broschi Farinelli (Naples 24/I/1705–Bologna 15/VII/1782)]. Someone governs [Eusébio]. Someone intones the word beauty [Baldassare Ferri (1610–1680), Antonio Maria Bernacchi (1685–

1756), Gaetano Majorano Caffarelli (1710–1783)], Gaetano Gua-
dagni (1725–1792), Gasparo Pacchierotti (1740–1821), Girolamo
Crescentini (1762–1848), Giambattista Velluti (1780–1861), Fran-
cesco Bernardi Senesino (ca. 1685–ca. 1759), Luigi Marchesi
(Milan 8/VII/1754–Villa Inzago 14/XII/1829), Alessandro Mores-
chi (Monte Compatrio 11/XI/1858–21/IV/1922), Domenico Mu-
stafà (Sterpara 16/IV/1829–Montefalco 17/III/1912), Giovanni
Cesari (Frosinone 25/VI/1843–Rome 10/III/1904)]. Does Someone swear? Does Someone look for the angle of the angel? The
question—obsessive. The absence (of an answer)—outrageous.
The eunuch. The berdache. The hijra. The castrato. Someone
pierced. Someone slithers. Slits. Someone takes the testicle, the
gonad, the genital organ. Does Someone take it? Someone penetrates. Someone mutilates. Desires.

There is a soothing terror when things slow. The world.

# 9

## The Adjective That Cuts

Eyes: big, inhabited, dark, close together, curious.
Hands: long, fine, bony, soft, amber-colored, pianistic.
Hair: salt-and-pepper, gleaming, short.
Mouth: flesh of my flesh, grooved, open, nervous.
Voice: from another world, level with the floor, sudden.
Sigh: emphatic, obvious, sexual.
Skin: weightless.
Beard: thick, trimmed, masculine.
Gaze: netlike, embracing, what do you want from me?
Question: is it you?

Sky: open, dry, jagged, blue.
Answer: sometimes.

Laughter: funny, cautious, deep, divine. A bird over a marble
tower.
Hand: on the shoulder, at the waist, caressing.
Wink: unexpected, angular, inclined.
Breath: lavender, Heno de Pravia, April wind. Mint. Childhood.
Laughter: interminable, discrete, approaching.
Gaze from afar: a bridge on the verge of collapse, a vine nearly

snapped, a cry for help, a woman tied to train tracks, an oracle, an investigation, a telescope.

Gaze from up close: a stabbing pain, a match, a burn, an ardor.

Stride: zigzagging, defaulting, dubious.

Question: is it my voice?
Answer: it is mine.

Noise: protective.

Alcohol: cold, banal, an anchor, a door, a button.

Voice: still from another world, distinct, multifaceted, deceitful, deep, guttural.

Hands: long, soft, bony, amber-colored, pianistic, on the iliac crests.

Order: follow me.

Fingernails: trimmed, clean, closed letters.

Mouth: full, open, eager, nervous, imperial, drooling, open wider, denotative, with nothing-beyond.

Hands: on the hands, against the wall, keys. Locks.

Breath: electronica music.

Gaze: boiling, netlike, skylike, nightlike.

Hands: in the sex on the sex under the sex behind the sex.

Chin: on the left shoulder.

Mouth: ah, the mouth. The ear. The neck. The hair.

Sex: the sex.

Question: is it your body?
Answer: and mine.

Intellectual interruption: only the hounding of death hurls us so furiously toward the unfamiliar body.

# 10

## The Tabloid Journalist

The Tabloid Journalist appeared in the doorway to my office on the last day of February. At first I thought it was a joke or an intervention organized by the theater students or by some feminist collective at the university. With big brown eyes, her hands weathered from unidentified though clearly manual labor, the woman with straight hair and jeans sat down facing my desk before proceeding to explain, with extreme timidity, with a sense of unmistakable shame, that she really was a journalist.

"Really?" I asked, unable to avoid the sarcasm.

"I always have to clarify. I'm assigned to the tabloid, so people don't think I'm qualified."

Her reasoning made sense to me, so I stayed quiet.

"I'm writing something about the case of the Castrated Men," she said with a quiet, almost faltering voice as she tried to hold my gaze.

"Something?" I asked again, thinking that the woman's shyness seemed pathological, almost unreal.

"A book," she said and looked down. "For myself," she added, "not for the newspaper."

*A book—for me, made by me—the journey of the consciousness through a state.* I thought about that fragment. I thought about those words by Caridad Atencio in Margaret Randall's translation. I thought about the arrogance or candor you'd need to say: I'm writing a book for myself. I thought about the discipline, the isolation, the foolishness you'd need to do such a thing. To write a book for myself, made by me. That's how I said it when you appeared on the other side of the door: a book for myself, made by you. And I repeated it several times as you smiled. And then I studied her again. The words didn't match the downcast face, the barely angular face, the just-past-adolescence face, malleable even, in front of me. And that not-fitting, that notorious discrepancy between the words and the voice that spoke them, left me perplexed.

"And you want to interview me?" I abruptly interrupted both her silence and mine because I couldn't believe that someone like her would *really* work for the tabloids. I couldn't believe that someone like her was *really* sitting behind a desk, in my office. "Do you want me to describe the body I saw again? Do you want me to share my list of suspects with you?"

"No," she said in the first firm tone I'd heard from her. "I want to talk about Alejandra Pizarnik."

Her answer surprised me.

"But not here," she added, "not now. I want you to think about it. I want you to think about whether you really want to talk about Alejandra Pizarnik."

*Really.*

When she stood up and turned her back on me, preparing to leave, I realized that the Tabloid Journalist's slight hump, caused more by bad posture than some congenital malformation, bore much of the weight of the world.

# 11

## The Poem Castrated by Its Own Language

The Detective called very early because she wanted to discuss the subject of castration in some poems by Alejandra Pizarnik. She said it just like that, without preamble or explanation; she said it literally, with an overtly neutral tone: I want to talk to you about castration in some poems by Alejandra Pizarnik.

"Over lunch?" I asked sarcastically, trying to underscore the poor taste entailed by bringing food to your mouth while talking, with that same mouth, about penises and testicles severed from their bodies. I couldn't understand why she sought me out so zealously; what good my answers would do.

"Yes," she answered, overlooking the malice in my remark. "The usual place?"

When I arrived, as with our previous meetings, she was already there, waiting for me. Her eyes fixed on the door, her fingers drumming nervously on the table. She could hardly wait for me to sit down before handing me the menu.

"Let's order," she said, treating the food as what it was, a mere pretext to our true main course—castration.

"So you still don't have any suspects?" I couldn't place why I was so eager to irritate her, but when she snapped the menu closed, I knew I'd succeeded. The Detective was not in a good mood.

"It's a difficult case," she explained, admirably maintaining her composure as she raised her hands and let them move, for the first time since I'd been meeting with her, with some sort of grace, some sort of emphasis in the air. "Full of psychological nooks and crannies. Of poetic shadows. Gender traps. Metaphors. Metonyms." And as she uttered the last word, she bowed her head, then looked up from that position. Her body facing down. Her eyes looking up. That clash of directions. I'd seen her do this several times before, but it wasn't until that moment that I understood it was her warning sign. Then the ironic smile appeared on her face: the thin corner that rose, in sync with her suddenly expressive hands, toward her temples.

"Transnominations," I murmured, settling into those words that weren't hers but mine. Feeling like an impostor of myself, I ordered a bottle of water from a busy waiter.

The Detective pulled some copies from her black briefcase. These partially wrinkled pages were printed with "On This Night in This World," the Pizarnik poem that was published, as she informed me just then, in the *Gaceta del Fondo de Cultura* in July 1972. The Detective placed the pages on the table. Pointing at the underlined passage, she asked: "So every poem fails?"

She was asking as if I were wondering the same thing. She asked with the kind of knowledge forged in strange and uncomfortable coincidences around a glass of water or a belt where countless suitcases circulate as if part of the same eternity. She asked with my words. This is a Great Kingdom that is missing a queen or a king. And I, for a moment, for just a second, believed we were understanding each other.

> on this night in this world
> words of the dream of childhood of death
> it's never what you wish to say

the mother-tongue castrates
the tongue is an organ of knowledge
about the failure of every poem
castrated by its own tongue
which is the organ of re-creation
of re-cognition
but not of resurrection.

I read carefully. I read with the kind of knot in my throat that's about to become a domestic animal. I read and had to pour myself the first glass of water. How could I tell the Detective that every poem is the inability of language to produce the presence in itself that, by simply being language, is all absence? How could I communicate to the Detective that the poem's task is not to communicate but quite the opposite: to protect the secret place that resists all communication, all transmission, every effort of translation? How could I tell her, without choking on the sip of water and the sadness that rose in me upon realizing, again and again, that the tongue will never be an organ of resurrection, that words, as Pizarnik says a few lines later, in a declaration no less gloomy for its accuracy, "do not make love / they make absence"? How could I explain to this woman, so firm, so well uniformed, that while she pointed her short immaculate fingernail to the word *castrated* in a poem about the uselessness, the inutility of all poems, all I could do was reminisce about the language that is all memory and, in being memory, is all absence, the contour of the body and the sex of that thin beautiful boy with a thick, manly beard, that had appeared, literally out of nowhere, out of the nowhere that is sometimes the absence of the absence of language, declaring, in the most jocular and lighthearted way, that he was Sometimes-Him? How could I not read aloud, in the most tremulous voice, "where does this conspiracy of invisibilities come from?" without causing that old shame she will never understand, the shame that isn't wounding her, as it wounds Pizarnik, in her "first person singular"? How could I tell the Detective to stop here, at these lines: "what did you do with the gift of sex? / oh, all my dead— / I ate them I choked / I've had enough of enough," read carefully, see for yourself, again and again, confirm it, and use the same informal command, again and yet again, do you see how one goes on "wasting the gifts of the body"?

But in the end I decided to ask you all that, because over time you learn to pose questions to someone who can actually answer them. Your silence, of course, filled me with pity.

"I just asked you, rhetorically, as you professor types say, if every poem is a failure," the Detective remarked with a certain tremor in her voice that became unequivocally hers. "It wasn't so you'd start crying, Cristina."

When she refilled my glass with water and placed it in front of me, I had to accept that, sooner rather than later, sooner than ever, the Detective and I were going to talk about poetry.

One day, without a doubt, we would.

# 12

## The Bearded Woman

The Man-He-Sometimes-Was placed a beard made from his own hair in my hands. That first exchange occurred under the domed, purple-painted ceilings of a movie theater that, over time, had been repurposed as a church.

"In the name of god," he murmured as he planted his hand on my neck and pulled me in. Oh, so cinematographic.

The kiss: anticipated, eager, thunderous, reactionary. Violent.

When I arranged the beard on my face, he pulled a little digital camera from his bag and asked me to pose by the saints, christs, angels. The list of his commands included:

1. Close your left eye.
2. Open your mouth.
3. Raise your arms.
4. Smile. (No, not like that.) (Like that.)
5. Pull up your shirt.
6. Turn around.
7. Pull down your pants.
8. Like that.
9. Don't pant.

And I saw his eyes again (dark, foolish, wet, nervous), and I thought it was the end of an eight-hundred-meter race in a location more than two thousand kilometers above sea level. I was going to smile. I was going to convert myself into a Lover with a Luminous Smile when I couldn't see his penis, lost inside my sex, which kept provoking pleasure. I stopped. I observed the domed purple ceiling. I returned to his eyes. Hands. Teeth. Beard. Knuckles. I kept going without being there. Torso. Bones. Pubic hair. Knees. His penis in those moments was mine. Then I smiled hermaphroditically. And the Man-He-Sometimes-Was spilled out in religious silence.

"That's what he got for disobeying his parents," he mused later with an air of feigned melancholy when we looked, still lying at the base of one of the long wooden benches, at the silent photographs.

# 13

## Where Once a Boy and a Girl Made Love . . .

*There are ashes and bloodstains and chipped nails and pubic hair and a bent candle once used for obscure purposes and sperm stains in the caked mud and condoms and a shambled house drawn in the sand and scraps of scented paper that were once love letters and the shattered glass ball of a fortune teller and wilted lilacs and severed heads lying on a pillow like impotent souls among the asphodels and cracked tables and old shoes and dresses in the mire and sick cats and eyes encrusted in a hand that slips away toward silence and other hands weighed down with signet rings and black foam spraying a mirror that gives no reflection and a young girl who suffocates her favorite dove in her sleep and black gold nuggets as resonant as gypsies in mourning who play their fiddles by the Dead Sea and a heart that lives for deception and a rose that blooms for betrayal and a boy crying in front of a raven that caws in the fields, and the muse puts on her mask to execute an inscrutable melody under a rain and it soothes my suffering.*

(On a page of Alejandra Pizarnik's collected poems, found at random)

(just after returning from the church that was once a movie theater)

(nine orders in my head)

(like that)

(purple)
(books know more than reality)

(not like that)

(crystal ball)
(poetry is not a place)

(like that).

# 14

## Denotative Desire

It was early morning when the Lover with the Luminous Smile told me the plot of his novel.

"More like a documentary," he corrected himself.

He would go out on the street armed with a video camera, big white posters, and colored markers. He would approach certain passersby—the strangest, the about-tos, the perfectly normal—and he would ask them to write on his posters what they were thinking in that very moment.

THEY'RE GOING TO FIRE ME AND I'M SCARED
WHAT DO YOU CARE?
NO ONE LOVES ME. I AM A MONSTER
WHAT TIME DOES THE FIRST STAR ON MARS COME
    OUT?
SELDOM THE LIPS
I WANT PEACHES

He would gather hundreds, thousands of similar phrases. He would film all of them. All without a voice. It would be a stellar moment of the unconscious. The antithesis of the public made in public. That impious paradox. That subtle contradiction. The social eruption of the intimate. One more triumph of writing.

When he finished recounting the plot of his documentary, he realized he was facing the window, his palms flat on the cold glass. A sleepwalker in his own head.

"I want to know everything," he said. Then he looked outside, and his eyes suddenly filled with fear. "Do you understand me?" he asked, turning around, confronting me.

It's difficult to understand what you do. Difficult to explain. Above all, this: it's difficult to explain. I saw him, but instead of seeing him I saw something else: another face: another body. I recognized the expression of suffering: the absence of the laughter that once illuminated everything in its path. The absence, even, of the lips. Of the mouth. Surely he didn't know how to whistle, he'd never done it. I identified the new gestures: the anxiety on the rims of his lower eyelids, the blue rage in the veins that gave a new shape to the backs of his hands. But I saw something else at the same time, another body. There was someone else, a slight presence in the aura his own body produced in the window reflection.

"You know everything," I managed to say, lowering my eyes. Seldom the shame. The guilt.

*Only death hurls us so furiously toward the unfamiliar body.*

"The poplars really are beautiful," he murmured later, much later, without turning toward me, blinking nervously, fluttering in himself. Then he went back to bed and fell asleep with his back to me. Dissipating.

# 15

---

## Authorship

The Tabloid Journalist who *really* was a journalist appeared in my classroom on the day we discussed the relationship between gender and creative writing. Some female students, especially those with straight hair and freckles, claimed there was something in this world that could be called "women's writing," and, elegantly, with incomparable disdain, cited works by French philosophers. Their accentless French, perfectly pronounced. The male students usually countered that it was nothing but the personal frustrations of frigid women writers or spurious pressures of the market and, as such, they defended a kind of literature—as they called it—without adjectives. There were of course female students who allied themselves in secret, or out loud, with the de-adjectivizing male students, especially those female students with literary ambitions and stubborn confidence in themselves. Or with a crush. There were also male students who ventured to speak, often with a certain timid stutter, about specifically masculine writing. Whenever we reached this point in the course, the same thing always happened. Friendships that had been slowly, painstakingly forged throughout the semester fell to pieces in the face of incredulity or intolerance, while others emerged from the sudden void of unexpected identification. I was prepared for everything. Used to positioning myself in the middle, not only did I let them talk, but I even asked them questions with which I hoped they'd conceive of or at least imagine the premise of the opposing argument. I am not a woman, I'd tell them, for example. And then I'd say the opposite. This is not the Kingdom of the Here. My voice, flat, moderate in volume, helped smooth things over when the discussion lurched along its own course toward insult. None of it was surprising or uncomfortable for me. It comes with the territory. The same as always. Except that this time the Journalist who *really* was a journalist broke—unintentionally, I'm sure—the rules of the game.

"And what is your position?" she asked without raising her hand or standing up. And I, who had noticed her among the students but hadn't paid much attention, turned to look at her, unable to hide my unease.

"I believe that is clear from the syllabus," I replied, adjusting my glasses on my nose and trying to change the subject.

"Well, it isn't clear to me. The readings"—and she raised all the copies—"represent the dominant points of view, even the opposing ones."

I looked at her again, curiously. There, sitting at a student desk, small, almost insignificant, was the woman who, days before, had struggled to maintain eye contact with me in my office. There was the timid woman I hadn't hesitated to dismiss as neurotic, demanding a categorical conclusion, the taking of a personal position. An answer.

"You write, I mean," she continued, lowering her voice. "You must have a position on this."

She spoke as if she were apologizing, but really, as she was wont to say, she really did not desist in her inquiry. She wanted an answer. She demanded an answer. She wasn't going to leave without an answer. The classroom, meanwhile, contracted in a cautious silence.

"Writers write," I said slowly, enunciating every word with the care employed by certain respectful foreigners as I arranged my books, as slowly as my enunciation, in the briefcase. "Not only about what they know about the world or themselves, but above all, fundamentally, about what they do not know about the world and about themselves."

I thought that would be sufficient, but I was wrong.

"Writers?" She repeated my phrase that indeed sounded, on her lips, though perhaps also on mine, hollow. "But you yourself," she insisted, "do you write as a woman?"

I laughed. I couldn't help it. I'm a goose in the Kingdom of the Outskirts. There, fixed by her intense, steady gaze, I let out a short burst of laughter that only by sheer force of will could I repress. Then came the silence. The expectation. The ellipses. Among all these things, a challenge was entertained, both tense and playful.

"Sometimes," I said very slowly. "Sometimes," I repeated, emphasizing, with full ludic intention, with my mind elsewhere, with my memory embedded in another body, the intermittence. I too was Sometimes-Her.

# 16

## Clear Light

At the beginning of March, on a day of clear light, the fourth man appeared.

Dismembered. No genitals. Covered in blood. A few young men who had gone camping on the outskirts of the city found him on the shore of a lake. When they got out of their truck, they noticed the smell and the buzz of flies behind the brush.

"There must be a dead guy over there," they'd said, with that premonition that sometimes comes with dark humor, the class clown.

When they approached and saw it, two of them vomited.

It took two others thirty or forty-five more seconds to put the pieces together and shape, from what was scattered on the ground, the body of a man. The puzzle of a body.

It was the youngest who called the police.

And then the terror and the clear light of early March became one.

They found the line from the poem later, during the first examinations. The Detective and the Detective's Assistant couldn't help but recognize the beauty in the phrase and the beauty in the composition of the phrase. And the macabre precision of the phrase: that beauty.

"It's true, death takes me in the throes of sex."

Each word drawn this time with the (elongated) (smooth) (flat) stones of the adjacent lake. Land art. Forms of procedural composition.

# 17

## I Didn't Try to Stop

The Tabloid Journalist caught up with me as I ran toward my apartment. The gravity, the anti-gravity. I'd changed my clothes in my office, leaving, once I was wearing my sneakers and sweatshirt, with a strange though real pressure on my chest. I assumed it was apprehension. I assumed it was sadness. I described it to you in these terms: this is called sadness here, within my Kingdom. And I wasn't ready to shut myself in an empty room with either one. The morning air, already warm and full of microplastics, didn't help. I ran not for pleasure, as I was accustomed to, but from horror. Quickly. Without cadence. Fleeing. I ran at your side. I realized I've been running by your side since day one. The slow motion of memory. The scattered breath that turned me inside out, placing my interior in everyone's ears. That's why when the Tabloid Journalist caught up with me. I didn't want to stop. I was startled by her frazzled, eager face. I was instantly sure it was a premonition. *The worst is to beg.*

She yelled my name before giving up. She asked me to pause. She said she had something to show me and held up a sheet of paper in her right hand. And I, bearing horror like a universal hand on my chest, didn't stop.

"You'll be sorry," she finally shrieked from afar. Motionless. Planted like a tree.

I didn't understand why or what I would be sorry for, but the threat was convincing. Real. So I ran even faster. I ran without looking back, guided only by the invisible hand squeezing my sternum. Once. Once and again. And again. When I got home, I poured myself a glass of water, still moving incessantly. Tremulous. A leaf. I paced back and forth, from one big window to another like a giant fly or a caged beast. Seldom the arms. I crashed against my own edges. I couldn't understand the deaths of those men. It broke my head. My hands. My knees. Seldom the lesion emerged, illuminated. I couldn't conceptualize the deaths of those men. And then I saw it all outside: an image of the Chapman Brothers. *Great Deeds Against the Dead.* And inside, Goya. Inside me, looking. *Nothing. The Event Will Tell.*

# 18

## Messages Under the Door

Everything would have stayed on track, which is often a track toward oblivion, if it hadn't been for the messages under the door. In the beginning of the era I called the era of the Castrated Men, there was nothing but a generalized apprehension that made me suspect everyone, especially lovers of contemporary art. Then, as the days went on, the indifference—impulsive, sagacious, cruel— emerged. As we know, it's impossible to live in a state of perpetual terror. As we know, when terror is permanent, the body finds or produces protective mechanisms among which the impossibility of feeling, the impossibility of paying attention, the impossibility of articulating nonsense, are frequent. I had already found myself in this stage of denial when I picked up the first message that appeared on my apartment floor.

I remember everything: it was cold, a cold that was quite unusual in April and for which, therefore, I had not prepared myself either physically or psychologically. I returned from my office as I always did, on foot, hurriedly, almost jogging, savoring the anticipation of my warm room, my silent ceilings, the surrounding calm. I opened the door then, in a state of total helplessness. That's how I saw it. I realized it. I went toward it. It was a sheet of bright white paper folded in four almost-perfect sections. The writing, in a dark reddish ink, an ink that looked as if it were made from a thick wine, from an almost blood-and-bone wine, was steady, stable, pretty. On that paper and in that ink, on one of the four almost-perfect sections, was my full name: cristina rivera garza. All in lowercase. Then, on the sheet, in handwriting that feigned calm, not haste, the message said:

"i want to talk to you. may i?"

The message, of course, was unsigned. In fact, it came without any identifying information other than the shape and color of the handwriting, the choice of lowercase letters, and the brevity of its challenge. *may i?* I asked myself for a long time. At a standstill. In a state contrary to anticipation. I asked myself silently and out loud. I asked myself and the window in which my reflection, distorted, asked me at the same time. I asked the landscape, confusing the evening poplars with tall European elms. may i? A long time passed in this very way.

# II

## The Traveler with an Emptied Glass

a)

I said that the first dead are our first masters, those who unlock the door for us that opens onto the other side, if only we are willing to bear it. Writing, in its noblest function, is the attempt to unerase, to unearth, to find the primitive picture again, ours, the one that frightens us.

b)

All great texts are victims of the questions: Who is killing me? To whom am I giving myself over to be killed?

c)

We are all dog-killers of the dog you are, killers of others. It is simply a question of designating the scene or scenes of *abandonment* that punctuate our paths so that they may be envisioned.

—HÉLÈNE CIXOUS, translated by
SARAH CORNELL and SUSAN SELLERS

# 19

---

## Message No. 2

I thought about it for many days. I thought about it when I first
saw your face in the tabloids. You were clearly beside yourself, and
despite that, or perhaps because of that, because of finding yourself undoubtedly beside yourself, you seemed like someone a person could converse with. Someone, that is, who knows how to
listen. Because in order to listen—did you know?—you will always
need to be a bit beside yourself. Beside Oneself. There was an attitude I can't describe in your decomposed features: a sort of inner
movement shifting naturally, willingly, outward. Opening up.
Toward me. Ever since the first time I saw you in the newspaper,
I yearned to talk to you, to fill time—which is sheer space,
intervened—with words and ears. Yours. Mine. At the end of the
day, no one really knows to whom words belong. I thought that if
I were to trust someone, I would trust someone like the woman-
beside-herself you were. Or me. But I already trusted myself. I
thought about it for many days, I suppose for full hours at a time,
with an obsession that those who know me would describe as
characteristic—although the day I finally did it, the day I picked
up the pen and wrote the message unwarrantedly fast, as if I'd
been told there were only three hours until the end of the world,
that day, as often happened to me, even though no one knew

about it, which meant that no one would suspect it was also characteristic of me, I couldn't think about it anymore. I stopped thinking entirely. Direct action. Everything outside me. Succinct. It was April, it's true. Early April.

May i? I asked you and you asked yourself, articulating the pronoun, the *I* that traveled from you to me and from me to you without any apparent qualms. You had the slip of paper in your hands and asked yourself again and again, may i?, forgetting you were exposed at the window, open, like it, to the world, observing the trees with a strange, still intensity. Sempiternal statue. Statue of wonderment. The paper was in your hands, and your gaze was fixed on the window as I watched you from a park bench, half-hidden among the shadows cast by the poplar trees, waiting anxiously, troubled, jubilant, for your verdict. May i? And I remained motionless as you didn't move, even trying to hold my breath. A statue like you. And I tried to identify the point on the horizon where your gaze was lost and where that same gaze found you again, full of haste, seized by urgency or fear, terrified, in any case, when you changed, however slightly, almost imperceptibly, your position. And I stayed silent as you did, too, for a long time. Hesitantly. And in the end—which is, as we both know, just one more variant of the beginning or, more precisely, of the beginnings—I smiled when you smiled, the weakest sunbeam illuminating your head for a fleeting instant.

My name is Joachima Abramović. And I do not know who I really am.

# 20

## Message No. 3

You shouldn't be afraid of me. I won't hurt you. I couldn't possibly hurt you. That's why I'll repeat it: you shouldn't be afraid of me. You don't have to glance over your shoulder like that, again and again, nervous, right after you turn the corner to your apartment or turn your back on the ancient building that houses your office. You don't have to rush to close, as if for the last time, the glass or wooden doors that your body goes through. I watch you, it's true, but with no other intention. I watch you to watch you. Besides, I've been watching you since before you knew you were being watched. Nothing has changed, really. Or, to be more precise, to strive for a certain kind of exactness, few things have changed since you became aware that I watch you. Things in general— have you noticed?—don't change much. Not much at all. I don't know if that should make me happy or sad, but it's clearly a fact. An irreversible fact. What little has changed between you and me is your awareness of me. Your learning of me. Your knowledge of me. Now you know I exist and that I call myself Joachima Abramović and that I watch you. That's all.

You know, of course, that I am not Joachima Abramović—but I'm sure, like me, you would like to be called this way. I'm convinced that if you were allowed to choose between the three-word name that adorns your office door and this other, foreign, incomprehensible, perhaps implosive name, with an accent over the c, you would choose the latter. And with this name on your tongue, you would look at yourself in the mirror and smile with sudden attraction to your image. That happened to me, Cristina. One day I found the name and I took it. And I looked at myself in the mirror. And then the vertigo forced me to release that burst of laughter that lived, without my knowing, in the wettest and deepest and darkest part of my stomach. Joachima, I said to myself. And Joachima I was. The Abramović came later.

Joachima Abramović, Cristina, is me. Have no doubt about it. And you are the woman who fears me; the woman who hopes to surprise me, and catch me, turning a corner or among the bustling crowd of a Saturday afternoon. You I am not. I are not you. Remember that. And stop being afraid already. Please. Truly, there's no reason to be.

# 21

## Message No. 4

My emptied glass is full of: gaps, silence, holes, margins, air.

There is a glass full of all this in my hands.

I constantly dream of it. I dream that, within my dream, there is someone like me with an emptied glass in their hands. And then I dream I walk inside that glass. And sometimes I leave the dream in which I walk inside my glass to wake up within the dream where someone like me walks on with an emptied glass in someone else's hands.

I dream a lot, Cristina. I dream that I call myself Joachima. I don't know how to stop the dreams. I don't know if I want to.

# 22

## Message No. 5

Their bodies are also destroyed in my dreams. I dream their penises are found—erect, invariable, cold—in glass jars that once contained preserves. And what could be more deserving of preservation than desire?

Sometimes I feel that desire. In my dreams. And I walk as if inside a glass toward the kitchen. There, I turn on the light, I cross the room to the wide white refrigerator with soft, rounded lines. An electrical appliance. Words in silver. I open it. More light. I look at bottles. I think. It takes me a moment to decide. One. Two. Three. Four. This time I choose the first. I carry it to the table, and slowly, as if this were the beginning of the satisfaction of desire, I turn the lid. The grinding. The smell of formaldehyde. The consistency of the stolen object. All of this in my hands and then in my mouth and in the blink of an eye between my breasts, over my navel, on my pubis, in my sex.

Do you think it means something, Cristina?

# 23

## Message No. 6

The detective woman will never understand me, Cristina. I swear she is incapable of that. The poor woman will never be able to even imagine someone like me. How many ways do you want me to spell it out for you? She doesn't have the mind for it. She doesn't take risks. She doesn't have enough violence inside her.

Stop calling her or meeting her at the same restaurant whenever you receive something from me. Don't you understand that I'm writing just for you? After all this, will you not be able to understand me either? Will you not be able to imagine me, either? Stop being afraid.

I'm letting you know, so you have fresh, disconcerting information to bring to that unimaginative woman who is slowly—do you see what I'm seeing?—trying to become your accomplice or your confessor; I'm letting you know that I no longer call myself Joachima Abramović.

Joachima Abramović died. Everything dies. You know that. And she died.

Now I am Gina Pane and I'm standing before a collection of razor blades on the bathroom shelf, right below the medicine cabinet mirror. The shelf is white. Have you ever carefully studied a razor blade? Even a simple razor blade becomes enigmatic when you observe it carefully.

From the outside: Gillette. Rectangular. With that curious shape in the empty center. Have you noticed that every center, when it is a center, is empty. Very thin. Sharp-edged.

From inside: A cut. A tiny thread of blood. A mark.

Every morning, before placing my body under the stream of the shower, I choose one. The selection takes a long time. Even though they look the same, they're really all very different. The difference, like all true difference, is millimetric. Only I can detect it. Only I am capable of imagining it. When I decide—and every morning I decide on one, no matter what—I bring it with me toward the water. A divine stream. If you were to do it, you too would notice the knife's soft precision as it slides over the skin, the blood's sinuous sensuality when it leaves the body, the irrefutable reality of the scar. You too would like it. I'm sure of that. I was sure of it as soon as I first saw your face, as I told you, in the tabloids. Beside yourself. You too would like this. My letter. The way the pen slides over the page, unsympathetically. And the ink's erotic gleam: brown, yes, mixed with wine. Burgundy. Try it. My ink. Your blood. This mark, Cristina. Unforgettable. You'll see. I call myself Gina Pane. And I just cut you.

P.S. Soon you'll have to confess that you meet that man in unspeakable places. Soon. You'll see. Nothing, dear, escapes HER gaze.

# 24

---

# Message No. 7

Dolls gutted by my worn doll hands—the disappointment that they're made of burlap (and your memory, a barren lap): the priest—it must be Tiresias—is floating down the river. But as for you, why did you let them kill you while listening to that story of the snow-covered poplars?

Nothing is hidden, Cristina. The signs are open. The phrase is open. Everything is broken. Split in two. In three. Dismembered. The body. The text. Everything is surface. A crack. Cut. Pause. See:

1) *Dolls gutted:* and is a man without a penis not a gutted doll?

2) *By my worn doll hands:* because, in truth, the doll is me. I am always the doll. What woman who is a woman is not the doll?

3) *The disappointment that they're made of burlap:* because it hurts so much, right, Cristina? to find out when you find out they're made of burlap.

4) *(and your memory, a barren lap):* ready for the scraps or for the fire.

5) *The priest—it must be Tiresias:* And did you know, Cristina, that Polyhymnia and Apollo visited Tiresias on his last night

to tell him he was a story and stories never end and stories create gods and poetry, never the other way around? Did you know that?

6) *Is floating down the river:* and everything does in the end. Float down the river. Which produces the river and the flow of the river.

7) *But as for you, why did you let them kill you while listening to that story of the snow-covered poplars?:* and have you realized, Cristina, that we're surrounded by poplars? They're so beautiful, aren't they? Definitely. They are. Really beautiful.

Those who analyze, murder. I'm sure you knew that, Professor. Those who read carefully, dismember.
We all kill.

This is a knife, not a joke.

If I could, I would tell you I'm in love. And now I'm Lynn. I call myself Lynn Hershman.

---

# 25

# Message No. 8

Lynn is wearing a felt hat. Lynn is wearing a wool coat with two pearl buttons on its fitted waist. Lynn is wearing white cashmere gloves. Lynn is walking slowly, swaying her hips. A woman from the fifties. The echo of her heels, clap, clap, clap, bounces off the concave ceilings of the convent. A photo. Lynn calls him. She says: come. Without saying anything. Lynn calls him and without saying anything says: come. A photo. Lynn pretends she's being followed and makes a face of alarm. A photo. Lynn lifts the back of her skirt and leans her breasts over a bench. Lynn looks up toward the tall, tall ogival window as she spreads her buttocks. A photo. Lynn gets comfortable and reads, uncomfortably, *Story of O*. Fabulous poplars outside. Air. Foliage. She sees this. Inside: the penis. Lynn squints. A photo. The penis penne-trates. Pen-'n-traits. Foliage. The penis disappears. Lynn closes her eyes. A photo. The forest.

And if this isn't sex, then what is?

And if this isn't death, then what is?

I called myself Lynn Hershman. But everything dies, Cristina. Remember? Everything tires.

Ay, Lynn, how I loved you. A photo. Another photo. The last one. Fin.

---

# 26

# Message No. 9

If this were a video I'd be here, in front of you, with my face covered by the image of a video. *Phantom Limb Seduction.* Did you know they keep hurting after amputation? You hurt me, for example. And I should hurt you. Ay. Ouch. Argh. I want to hurt you. Clenched teeth. Hands like fists. The hint of a true tear in a corner of the eye. Something like that.

If I had a body, a full body, a unit, not this agglomeration of phantom members, I would also be here, in front of you. Then I'd tell you that I call myself Roberta, that I call myself Tillie. I'd tell you I like poplars. I'd tell you that Mary Shelley was the first woman to create the idea of an artificial human. I'd tell you that Frankenstein is an enigmatic being. I'd run at your side. I'd always run.

If it were an emptied glass, I would place it here, inside your sex.

If I wrote you messages, I'd surely confess to it. I'd say: Leave me alone. I'd say: It already was. And I'd let myself be cursed for the way the wine ink opens furrows on the 100-percent white cotton page. And I'd fold the paper, crick crack crack, and running at your side, always at your side, always close to you, a phantom limb, I'd deposit it in unexpected but obvious places.

The noise of the breath. Listen to it. The clumsy beat. The open mouth. Register all of it.

I know you better than you know yourself. And I boast about it. That's what I would say if I met you. That's what I would say if you'd ever seen me: eyes frightened but blue, long fingers, curly hair, boy's hips. If you'd ever approached me with outstretched arms and a bright smile. I know you better than you know yourself. If you knew my name.

If this were a video. If it had a body. If it were an emptied glass. If it wrote. If I were an incredible shrinking woman. My name is Lynn. Lynn Hershman. And my name, as you can imagine, as you well know, as is true of you too—my name is not me.

# 27

---

# Message No. 10

So you like May? May isn't now, Cristina. Understand that. How many ways will I have to spell it out for you? May was.

No one would die in May.

I'm leaving you this page under your shoe, stuck there with chewing gum. You'll walk. You'll take only two or three steps and you'll notice. You'll rip it off with a sudden, desperate jerk. You'll read me. You'll have no choice. You'll run off like always. But the pain will make you realize that these aren't your running shoes. The pain in the upper part of your heel. This pain.

This is a joke, not a razor, Cristina. But what could be more harmful than a sense of humor? What cuts more than a word?

I would never hurt you. Not in May. Because May was.

When you stop, I want you to think this: Think that someone is observing you from the only place you cannot see. Think that you have no way out. And then, after you've thought all this, think—and think about it carefully—think that I will always love you.

# 28

## Message No. 11

Elizabeth: A name.

*The sexual act: a sort of zone enclosed by a circle.*

Everything is possible. Everything should be possible. Even talking with you.

May i?

"And so I must tell you, devoted readeresses, that if you keep reading me so closely, I'll stop writing. In short, at least pretend."

Nothing matters that much, not even a penis. Your detective should know that. Stop playing hide-and-seek already. Start playing already.

NOTHING FUNNIER THAN THE UNFULFILLED DESIRES OF OTHERS.

Elizabeth Báthory: A name and a last name.

Neither is mine.

*A storm: feeling yourself spelled out by someone semiliterate.*

Something like that.

Something like that: my life with you two. Something like that.

---

# 29

# Message No. 12

This is my last message. Forgive me, but I get sentimental. I can't with the two of you; you're a real pain. That's why I'm stopping. Because you two won't.

I'm leaving the page stuck to your window, on the outside, so that when you walk in with the unimaginative woman, right when you both freeze with shock and fear, you'll think that I could be a man who cleans windows in tall buildings, or that I could be a mechanical bird, or that I'm you, Cristina, or her. The Detective.

Now you're pausing, right? Now you're getting closer. Now you're placing your hands on the glass (like you do, sometimes, like you do, some nights) without touching it. The message is untouchable. You just discovered it. The message is untouchable. The message is on the other side of the glass.

I'll leave you, then, with your suspicion.

(Yes, this is a laugh. This is, indeed, a cackle. Yes.)

# III

## The Detective's Mind

Regarding death in the first person—that is, my own—I can say nothing at all, as it is my death. I take my secret, if there is such, to the grave. That leaves death in the second person, the death of someone close, which is the highest form of philosophical experience because it is tangential to two people who are close to each other. It is the most like my own without being my own, and without being in any way the impersonal and anonymous death of the social phenomenon. It is someone else, not me, so I will survive. I can see him die. I see him dead. It is someone else not me; and at the same time, it is what touches me most closely. Beyond that would be my death, it would touch me. The philosophy of death is made for us by its proximity.

—VLADIMIR JANKÉLÉVITCH

# 30

## What Do You Need to Kill a Man?

First there's the moan. A few moans. Then the quick but almost imperceptible fluttering of the eyelashes. Tiny creases around the eyes. Two or three stammered sounds. Perhaps the beginning of a word, a phrase. A bead of sweat. A trace of saliva at the corners of the lips. The echo of all that. The head on the pillow. The tangled hair. The moan again. The saliva. Later: the dawn. Something full of sun.

(Someone sleeps.)

Finally able to open the eyes, in the second preceding the wakefulness that is no longer sleep, the images of the dreamlike story swiftly appear:

It's nighttime. It's a hot, noisy night. She's crouching behind a truck, protecting herself. The beating of her heart. The crazy beating of her heart. There are screams. And the noise that can be heard is the noise of the bullets, their trajectory. Their long flight through the air. A lightness. Their final target. This is the moment: she stands up, not looking, unable to see anything, prisoner to her heart's wild beating, takes the revolver in her hands, and aims it into the immense night. Into the night. Then everything calms down, all at once. And the noise of the silence is more voluminous than the noise of the violence.

She says: you don't need to do anything but aim into the night.

She doesn't really say it. She babbles it. This: you don't need to do anything but aim into the night to kill a man.

Then she meets her gaze again. The gaze of the suspect. The gaze of the woman who very well could have killed a man, then three more. Violently. A tunnel there. An entrance orifice without an exit orifice. The empty riverbed. Could it have been her? The gaze that looks back at her in turn, attentive. Without blinking. The gaze that accuses her. The gaze that asks itself the same question: Could it have been her? Then she remembers the full list: *A man who cleans windows. A mechanical bird. You yourself. The Detective.* She smiles. She uncovers herself. She jumps down from the bed to the floor. The creak of waking up. She dreamed something. She wants to remember it now but can't. She dreamed something that won't let her wake in peace.

# 31

## Defeat
## Wring Out
## Throw Away

What's visible:

The Detective dances alone. She barely sways. She gently bends her knees. She barely dances at all, really. She half closes her eyes and half opens them. She takes a swig from the beer in her left hand. She closes her mouth. A grimace. She's standing close to the bar, far from the little stage where four skinny musicians play a raucous number. She's far from the crowd that jumps and shakes to the rhythm of their songs. But she's there. She winds the ends of her hair around her index finger. And she isn't there. Another swig of beer. Furrowed brow. Total concentration. The concentration of someone trying to forget something else. There, at the edge of a room full of people, besieged by limbs and sweat and sounds, the Detective looks like a lighthouse, something erect and tall that illuminates what happens around it and at its feet. Down below. A giantess. Another swig of beer. But when she looks up, when she beholds what's around her with a severity that reads as intolerance or disdain, it seems obvious that the Detective's lighthouse doesn't illuminate her surroundings; it obscures them. All that exists is what she thinks, everything else remains in darkness. It's a bar. A place where she has found a corner, a fold, a refuge.

A dark place where a woman who is thinking about something else barely dances. Something more.

When she leaves the place, she stuffs her hands into her pockets and strolls, zigzagging, along the nighttime sidewalks. The light sound of her steps. The sudden leap over the tracks. The wind through the fronds.

What's invisible:

She thinks about the dead men. One, Two, Three, Four. She thinks about those mutilated bodies that are no longer just a case or an event or an alarming news story but also, and above all, a loss. Something unique. She thinks about their many hands, their sobbing relatives, their weekends, their shoes. She thinks about the final moment. Where were they going when they were really headed toward death? Who was left waiting for them? The scream or the sigh. She thinks about the noise they made to show the world they understood: this is the end. Their eyes blank? A curse or a plea in their mouths? She knows their names and she remembers their faces, but in order to work on their cases she needs to call them One, Two, Three, Four. That way they don't make her want to vomit. That way she protects them. This is a veil. One, Two, Three, Four. That's what she calls them when she sits down at the table and, instead of eating, thinks. She remembers. She classifies. She enumerates. She chews.

One. Two. Three. Four.

How many times will she betray them? she wonders there, within everything that cannot be seen, behind her eyelids. She knows she won't stop when she needs to go where the gun went: she'll sniff inside the body just like the murderer, and unlike the murderer, she'll kill them a second time. Subtle discrepancy. She'll scour their life. She'll turn them over and then to the right. Dirty clothes. She knows she'll open their eyes (a lamp) (a microscope) and ask questions and examine the context with meticulous calm. Discipline. So many years of experience. One, Two, Three, Four. She wants to protect them from everything, especially from herself. She wants the dead men, already dead, to die truthfully. For them to rest in peace, that's what she wants, and that's what she cannot give them, she thinks. Both anonymous and divine, the dead men. Intact. That's how she wants them. She doesn't want to draw back the veil she must draw back the veil. One, Two, Three, Four. The Detective must regard the information as a complete unit in order to identify the contrast, the similarity. A behavioral pattern. She needs to know she doesn't want to know she will know. She'll carve them up again. She'll display them, smugly, on the clean table of a page. She'll crown herself with dead men, that's what she thinks. One, Two, Three, Four. The oblique smile on her face. That sadness. The Detective must wring out those dead finish those dead torture those dead to find the thread that ties them to their executioner. That's what embarrasses her: having to kill the bodies she examines. Doing it with such exactitude, such rage:

|  | One | Two | Three | Four |
|---|---|---|---|---|
| Age | 28 | 32 | 35 | 27 |
| Marital status | Single | Single | Divorced | Married |
| Occupation | Journalist | Librarian | Translator | Teacher |
| Nationality | Local | Local | Foreigner | Local |
| Height | 1.72 | 1.64 | 1.74 | 1.69 |
| Skin tone | Brown | White | Brown | Brown |
| Eyes | Brown | Black | Brown | Brown |

What's written on a loose sheet of paper:

*When, at midday, at the end of one of our usual meals, the De-tective asked, "Don't you think that woman or that man writes a lot like you?" As she held the messages from the Traveler with an Emptied Glass in her hands, I was sure the distrust was mutual. I didn't ask which books she'd read, nor did I ask for examples. I didn't defend myself. I didn't say "Don't you think you're talking more and more like me?" squinting. Instead I entertained myself by watching the smooth flight of a fly. Instead I thought to my-self, since I didn't need any kind of explanation, that writing like someone else or talking like someone else isn't all that improbable in the end. Or that difficult. And I remembered, as I listened with heightened attention to the buzzing of the fly that collided repeat-edly with the windowpane, how some of the writing exercises I'd done as a little girl—exercises that at first involved literally tran-scribing full paragraphs from my favorite books on bright white, one-hundred-percent cotton pages, and which eventually involved imitating certain stylistic markers—the way some dashes split open the territory of the subordinate clause, the rhythm set and followed by periods, the slow conclusion a comma can invoke—until, once tamed, once defeated, once wrung out, I felt I had the right to throw away the style as well as the writing of that style, so beloved and so despicable at once. I turned to look her in the eye and there, met with her open gaze, I wondered how long it had taken the Detective to get there. To defeat me. Wring me out. Throw me away.*

*The fly then alighted on the rim of a glass of wine. And I de-cided I'd better concentrate instead on that new form of silence.*

What's audible:

There is a labyrinth and within the labyrinth there is a man walking alongside a bough. It could be from a willow but it's from a birch, the bough. Anyway, what matters is the sound of the footsteps (patent leather shoes, white sneakers, sandals) and the sound of the leaves and the sound of the breath when it ends.

What's really happening:

This the novel cannot know.

# 32

## The Spectator Must Be Here and Now

Marina Abramović said she was interested in art that disturbs its viewers and sparks a moment of danger. As such, she added, the audience has no choice but to live in the here and now. She said: You have to let the danger aim at you, that's the idea—to place yourself in the target of the now.

As she reads, the Detective pronounces the word *Belgrade*. She does it so many times that the word eventually loses its meaning. *Belgrade.* Now the word is just a light concatenation of letters. Barely a chain of sounds. A dismemberment in the making. Just like that, without unity, without completeness, the word pleases her. She must like it enough to feel pleasure when uttering it, when hearing it enunciated, beyond herself. *Belgrade.* Marina Abramović was born in Belgrade.

The question the Detective writes slowly, very slowly, on a sheet of graph paper in her Italian-style Bond notebook:

*Why would someone want to be Marina Abramović? Why would someone, the writer of anonymous letters, choose that name of all names? That work?*

What the Detective sees while studying a windowless wall, turning her back to her desk:

1) A woman sits in a room for more than four days to clean fifteen hundred beef bones while singing lullabies. In the same place, three projectors show idyllic scenes of the woman with her parents. The woman doesn't stop singing. She doesn't stop.

2) An open hand on a table. A knife between the index and middle fingers. Between the thumb and index finger. Between the pinky and ring fingers. Between the middle and index fingers. Drops of blood between them all. The speed perceived. The sound. The sound. The sound. The sound. The real sound and the recording of the sound. All this repeated ad nauseam.

3) A woman embarks on a two-thousand-kilometer walk from the far end of a wall. A man does the same thing from the other end. Ninety days later, the man and the woman meet in the middle of the route. A date at the end of the world. Then the woman keeps walking. The man too. A brutal separation. All this at Èrláng Shān on June 27, 1988.

4) A woman cleans a skeleton with water and a brush. Thoroughly. With attention to detail. With tenderness, even.

5) A woman hurts herself. In public.

6) A woman sitting, for more than four days, in a room suffused with the stench of raw meat and images of her childhood. A woman who sings incessantly. Her long black hair. The grimace of childhood. Her tears.

7) The fingers of the open hand. Fragile and orphaned, the fingers. The sound of the tip of the knife digging into the wood of the table. Over and over again. Again. The speed.

8) A woman embarks on foot to travel, in the opposite direction, all the kilometers needed to say: this is a separation.

9) A body says: the body suffers.

10) A body says: everything is a moment of danger.

11) A woman sits down in the middle of a room, and as she rips raw flesh from the bones of cows, as she cries and sings, as she fights the urge to vomit, she watches projected images of a body that stands up behind a vehicle and, reaching out its right hand, aims into the night. The smell of the dead man all around. The first smell of the body.

12) A woman travels an enormous distance, two thousand kilometers, half a country, to say: this is a separation.

13) A woman lies naked behind an immaculate skeleton.

14) A woman puts on a blue uniform and pulls back her loose hair. The open hand. The swift knife. The revolver. The

night. Fifteen hundred beef bones. A lullaby. The great
wall of China. All the walls. A woman. The danger.

What the Detective says when a young man grazes her shoulder
once, twice, three times:

"Valerio, what do you want now?"

# 33

---

## We're All in the Loop Here

She's always surprised by the silence of his approach. She can't say whether it's excessive shyness or childhood habit or just his bone structure, but Valerio finds a way to make his presence a perpetual apparition. A reason to shudder. She once heard the phrase: an apparition is always an apparition. Whenever she looks at him like that, startled, she wonders whether he's been working for her for a short time or a long time, and in every instance, no matter how hard she looks at him and tries to do the math, she must accept that she doesn't know the answer.

"Anything important?" she asks, returning her attention to the computer screen.

"We still haven't found the weapon," he ceremoniously recites, as if he weren't the bearer of bad news. "Or the penises. We have the forensic report: nothing surprising. And we have this," he says, placing a pile of newspapers on her desk, "as well."

The Detective takes in the headlines, lips pursed, and looks at him again.

"I thought this was about something important." The fingers of both hands on the keyboard, pressing letters.

"There's something," he murmurs after a long pause, taking a seat across from the desk. "A sort of route."

Before continuing, he extracts a little map from his pocket and uses a red pen to circle the addresses of the victims' homes in the suburbs of the city. Then, with the same pen, he marks an X on the very central spot where their lifeless bodies turned up.

"Do you see it?" The anxiety in his clear, tremulous, arrogant face.

"Really far from their natural territories, yes," the Detective confirms. "Quite far."

"They're men in search of something, don't you think?" he says aloud, but addressing himself, not her. "They all left the comfort of their homes or apartments or lofts—and I can assure you that all their homes are truly comfortable—for downtown in hopes of finding something." He cuts himself off, looks up at the ceiling, trying to identify the word that would let him say what he thinks, but when he can't, he parsimoniously meets the Detective's eyes again. "Something different. A risk, perhaps."

"Not necessarily to find something, Valerio," she rebukes him. "They also could have left the suburbs to lose something. To get lost. After all, why else would someone go downtown on a weekend night except to get lost?"

Bent over the desk, her gaze fixed on the young man as he tries to find an illegible word on her office ceiling, the Detective looks like an eagle. A bird of prey.

"I already interviewed the bartender where the first man spent his last night." He pauses, waiting for the Detective's question; when it doesn't come, he continues without any apparent affront. "He went out alone. He'd been there a couple hours. Looking, mostly."

"Looking for what?"

"Sex, of course," he says, both incredulous and annoyed. "Vulva. Anus. Ass. Lips."

The Detective looks him up and down.

"Are you sure?"

"About what?" he asks, visibly exasperated.

"That that's what he was looking for," she answers with a terse calm, her voice barely contained. "He could have been looking for all sorts of things in the end."

"Indeed," he murmurs with a barely veiled sting in his voice, both fed up and uncomfortable. "In any case, you should probably review those." He signals the pile of newspapers with the flick of his eye. "One of them insinuates that once, in self-defense"—he whispers at first. Met with her lack of reaction, her indifference, the gaze that flees toward the screen, he raises his voice—"they accuse you of killing a man."

The Detective grabs the newspaper and finds herself inundated, before she starts to read the text her Assistant is pointing to, by a series of swift and confusing images. There is the woman crouching behind the bed of a truck. There is the night and, in the night, the whistle of bullets cutting across it. There she is, she herself, suddenly straightening up before all that and shooting, her heartbeat in the trigger, into the night. The silence is also there. The subsequent silence. The immediate silence and also the silence of many years together. It's her recurring dream. Her nightmare. She stands up and paces briefly around her chair, a caged animal, before falling into it again, exhausted. It is, of course—now she recognizes it perfectly—her nightmare. That's what she's been dreaming. Those are the images that won't leave her in peace, night after night, in the few hours she can manage a fragile, dread-filled sleep suffused by the whistling of the bullet, that heartbeat, the dark.

"You know I was exonerated of all these charges, right?" Her index finger on the newspaper letters, her eyes bright with a gleam he doesn't recognize. For a moment he thinks the Detective is about to cry or split in two or shatter into a thousand pieces. A ticking time bomb. For just a moment he convinces himself that the woman with whom he has worked for a couple months without ever asking her any personal questions, without ever sharing any private information of his own, has, indeed, days and nights, minutes, hours, saliva, a past. She is a human being, he thinks. For the first time . . . And the mere silent thought puts him in a good mood.

"Of course," he says. "We're all in the loop here."

## 34

You'll Never Find Anything
Strange Here, Miss

The gaze of a mother who has lost a child, especially if that child
has suffered a violent death, is unlike anything else in the world.
That gaze holds no metaphor, no analogy, no metonymy. Strictly
speaking, it is a gaze that does not exist. On the doorstep, her head
cocked slightly to the left, the Detective thinks about the one she
knows so well, the nonexistent gaze she's seen so many times, seconds before the mother of the first murdered man opens the door.

Then it happens: she sees it. The mother's gaze collides with
her own body and upon colliding, creates it. There is no noise.

"I was waiting for you," says the woman. And it's true. There are
cups of tea and cookies on the coffee table. A smell of chrysanthe-
mums. Another of fresh laundry. Except for the look in her eyes,
the Mother appears normal: a middle-aged woman who tends to
her family and puts a lot of effort into keeping up her house. Silky
hands. Manicured nails. Curls. Except for the fact that they're
preparing to talk about her murdered son, her brutally castrated
son, the woman seems normal. The Detective observes her without blinking and listens to her with the professional distance and
impartiality she's been able to manufacture over the years: emo-
tionless but empathetic, uninvolved but conveying human concern, integrity. Strength. The Mother speaks to that person who

listens. She does it tentatively, quietly, whispering. She does it and touches her hands together, one to the other, as if they were seeking refuge or solace. One, two tears escape her. In spite of her. Just then, as the woman opens up, the Detective identifies it: the new wrinkle. It's barely a line on her chin; a line that only appears with certain phrases, the most broken or barren. The least audible. The Detective pauses on the edge of her seat, trying to understand the Mother's words without interrupting her story, and so she studies her closely and can't help but recognize it: it's the wrinkle born the day after the death was announced. She knows it well. It's a wrinkle that comes, whole and swift, from violence: the violence of death, the violence of the knowledge of death. It's the skin's response.

To avoid looking at the wrinkle that suddenly pains her, the Detective moves as far away as possible from the Mother's face, but she soon finds, at this greater distance, that she can't hear the answers she has come looking for. So she moves closer again, although she tries to distract herself this time by looking sidelong at her surroundings. What she sees in this way, obliquely, the reflection of a reflection, shakes her. She doesn't know why, but the order of the house, its neutral colors, its fluffy carpet, distresses her, as did the chin wrinkle only moments before. The innocence of the space. The white breadth of the space where a boy grew up before he was found mutilated many years later. The contrast ruffles her. That's why she observes the Mother, blinking noisily, and then can't keep looking at her. She lowers her gaze and thinks, instead of paying proper attention, about her own mother's eyes. About the wrinkle she also bears on her chin. Will she look at her like that one day? she wonders, feeling immediately pathetic, then gives the hint of a smile, looks up, and prepares to listen.

The Mother talks about her son's youth. She talks about his beauty. She talks about his brown eyes. And she daydreams: childhood, those years; the years when no one imagined what would happen, what was happening right then and there, the reason for the meeting between the Mother with the nonexistent gaze and a Detective accustomed to hearing unspeakable things. She talks about his sense of humor. About his way of walking: always hurried, confident. She talks about the first articles in the press and shows her yellowed clippings, folded in half, fragile. The smell of dust. The cough. No dangerous topics. Nothing out of the ordinary. Things of the time. She talks about someone she will love, hopelessly, for the rest of her life. Alert and respectful, the Detective allows the information to accumulate. She should say something, perhaps something that's already been said, something to help her reassemble the story that she must now untangle, eviscerate.

E-viscera-te.

The image comes immediately with the word itself, e-viscera-te: there it is again, the thrashed belly, open, still covered in fresh blood. A mouth, really. A brutal orifice. The visceraless. The viscera exposed.

"But you must have some idea by now, right?" the Mother asks when she realizes that the Detective, if just for a few seconds, has been distracted by something else. Something intangible.

"Nothing concrete," she confesses. "That's why you need to talk. Talk to me."

The Mother brings out photos: a newborn, a boy, a teenager, a man. Linear development. Curve of life.

The Mother tells her: schools, friends, trips, interests, hobbies.

The Mother hypothesizes: a robbery (it doesn't make sense), an accident (it doesn't look like it), revenge? (but for whom?)

The Mother suddenly falls silent. It seems she has just realized her son is dead, dead forever. Then she buries her face in her hollow palms and sobs noisily, not caring that the Detective is watching her, contritely, at close range.

"I know how difficult this moment is"—she clears her throat—"but it would help if you could speak about his final days. Your son's last days. Any sudden change? Any unexpected behavior?" The two look at each other, a collision of missing information: the slight tremor of anxiety. The fear.

"What enemy could hate him enough to commit such a brutal act, officer?" she asks, not trying to answer a question she hasn't fully heard. "Who couldn't know that the enemy, his enemy, was capable of this and maybe more? Who could be so blind, so deaf, so mute?" Her voice rises in volume with every question. "Who was my son, really?" An empty dune in each inordinately open eye.

There was the forbidden question again. This is the question with which the acquaintances and loved ones admit to what everyone else can see when a murder takes place: they didn't know him. Not entirely. Not in the way they believed. He was Another. He is Another. He always was Another. That's what murder does. With its weapons, which aren't metaphorical, a murder uncovers the underground history in the Victim's life story. It lifts the curtains. It opens the doors. It lowers the veil. It turns on the light. Lays bare: that's what murder does. Behold. Open.

"My son was happy," the Mother says, as if happiness were a shield against death or against knowing what the enemy is capable of. "I can assure you that my boy was happy," she insists.

"Do you know if he liked contemporary art?" the Detective asks after a long silence.

The Mother looks back at her, open-mouthed, red-eyed, the ends of her hair sticking up, suddenly electrified.

"I don't know, Officer," she finally murmurs. "I don't know what contemporary art is," the woman admits in a whisper before succumbing to a silence full of childhood memories. His childhood. Her child. Her only son. The Detective then asks if she can see his old room, and the mother meekly leads her upstairs without another word. The stench of things unmoved and stored as soon as the door opens. The rigid scene of an unmined field before her eyes. The blue walls. The blue curtains. The books on the shelves. The little desk under the window. The screen of a small television. The video game cables. The Detective absorbs it all as she steps over the carpet. It's the clean, orderly room of a happy boy, a boy like any other. It's the room she never had. She turns to look at the Mother, who rests her cheek, exhausted, against the doorframe.

"You're never going to find anything strange here, miss," she murmurs as the Detective pauses in the middle of the bedroom, still undecided whether to open the drawers or the closet doors.

"I know," she responds. Her eyes half-shut. Her voice soft. "I know," she repeats, glancing at her again.

When the Detective leaves that spacious white house, that orderly blue room, she can't help but notice she is clenching her fists. Before turning the car on, however, she doesn't know that she'll turn right instead of left two blocks from here, and that, instead of heading toward her office, she'll take the fast lane, only to emerge minutes later on a narrow street sown with traffic lights. Under one of them, anxiously waiting for the change from red to green, the Detective realizes she's about to pass the Alley of the Castrated Man. Without stopping there, she slows down, down to a crawl, and turns in to alleyways riddled with potholes and lined with bustling sidewalks. It's dusk. The sunlight has a violet tint that forces her to notice the shapes of the clouds. It isn't until she switches off the engine that she accepts it: she has parked very close to her mother's house. She wants to see her without being seen. She doesn't want to enter that dark, narrow apartment where she's currently making dinner. The smell of frying oil in the air. The onion. The pepper. The dirty apron. She doesn't want to see her sweet big eyes or feel her embrace or sit down at her table. Most of all, she doesn't want to walk past the bulge of the man, legs spread, his arms wide across the couch, as he watches the television while he burps or indiscreetly scratches his testicles. She wants to peer through their windows and trawl, if possible, for some echo of her voice, but she doesn't want to go in. Not into that. Not into that world. Instead, she rolls down the windows of her car and cranes her neck to see if there, in that other window, her mother's silhouette might suddenly appear. A shadow of her face.

"You should come in," she hears them say. She hears it clearly.

"I know," she responds. "I know," she insists. Then she turns the engine on again, and just as she came—at a crawl, with the levity of the impossible beings—she moves away from the red brick buildings behind which her mother. Her father. Her dog.

"I should," she murmurs when she can finally speed up. "I know. I know what I should do."

# 35

## The Spectator

She doesn't know whether she goes back because she's interested in seeing the scene of the first crime again or because she wants to see the tattooed eyes in her eyes. Someone leads her by the hand, pulling her. When she pauses, when doubt or fear paralyzes her legs, Something or Someone whispers words in her ear: They say: *I'm talking about that bitch who sits in the silence weaving a plot.* It says: *If I am anything, it is violence.* It says: It does not mean *to go meet someone* but rather *to lie there because someone doesn't arrive.* She lets herself be led from time to time, and from time to time, she suspends herself again. She looks at the sky. She watches the passersby. She watches the apparitions. I'm the one lying there, she thinks. She watches the evening light. Standing before a store window, she finds she has become, in that very moment, an illuminated woman. Pure interior.

"I'm a metal girl, can't you see?" she hears someone say. "I swear I'll close my eyes and I'll never find relief."

The noise of the engines distracts her. The explosion of the ignition. The slow distance of the engine. The trajectory of the machine as it moves away.

"It's hard to breathe here," she hears, and as she too is struggling a bit to inhale and exhale, she immediately sits down. She tilts her head to the right and breathes deeply, as deeply as she can, before pulling a coin from her pants pocket. She looks at it, plays with it. Then she scrapes it along the wall, leaving her mark. A long line. A fragile line. When she looks back, the light surprises her.

"Don't follow me," she murmurs, annoyed.

"I told you, I'm a metal girl."

She holds a map in her hands. She's afraid and looks at the map, trying to orient herself or hide her eyes or pretend she's a person who needs a map to walk. It's the map of a city marked by crosses. Each cross is a signal that means: THE BODY OF A CASTRATED MAN WAS FOUND HERE.

As she walks, she establishes that this is a small-scale city with an angular design. It's a city made up of side streets, not streets; a shadowy city that only rarely receives the shine of artificial light. A city built with bricks—red, coarse, crumbling—not smooth blocks of concrete. It isn't an iron city. It isn't a city soft to the touch. It's easier to hear it or smell it than to see it. The city lives within the other city that contains it, in its very core, but also on its unexpected internal shores—in the urban islands where a natural world, dry and contained, expands in outright competition with the context that hosts it. She looks at the map again and immediately turns to look at her surroundings. More than a place, it's a displacement, she tells herself. And more than a displacement, it's the obstacle or the doubt that interrupts the displacement or breaks it up, she tells herself. The singular city, the city of the dead, the city whose scaled reproduction she now holds in her hands while she moves through its viscera, is above all a way of hesitating with the feet, with the whole body. With the body in motion. What she has in her hands is the map of a walker's city, she tells herself. The murderer or the murderess is more than anything else a good walker.

The Detective's body penetrates the territory of this enclosed city. The image of a boat's keel when it breaks through the already churning waters of a lake. The image of the tongue when, in the fluid contact of the kiss, it slips into the foreign mouth. Outside. Inside. A transition. There are only blurry images for that, but she sees them anyway. More a daydream than a reflection. More a dazzling. A sudden loss of reason.

It's a teenage girl: knees protected by oval patches on the jeans: mint-flavored gum: dark glasses: speed in the steps that cross the road: chewed nails: all kinds of scratches. The teenager enters the city, founding it. Everything exists in relation to her: the rectangular buildings whose walls reveal two or three layers of old paint, flakes of decay. *Hey you, get down from there.* Windows like holes: curtains like screens: light from televisions behind all that: dirty noise. *What do you think you are? Immortal?* Women slowly strolling. Men quickly striding. The gray: the color gray and the gray itself: the starry night skies. *I'm going to tell your mother.* Rooftop terraces where a body trying to escape curls up. Notebook on knees. The words: *I'm not from here. I am not from here. I'm not from here. I see more.*

The Detective pauses, cautious, and steps aside when she sees her pass.

The long-haired teenager whispers it, between her teeth, many times. *I'm not from here.* And then, as if there were no alternative, *I'm never coming back. I'm leaving and I'm never coming back.* And while she utters it, she leans over the notebook like a beggar, hands pressed to their face, staring in at the set table through a wide, wide window. The salivating mouth. The resentment. The desire for revenge. The pencil crosses the page, wounding it. The teenager says it again and again, more emphatically every time. *I will be another. I will become another.* And she looks at everything then like someone saying goodbye. Like someone already gone.

A flock of birds forces her head skyward: night is about to arrive. The cold startles her awake. She has to take in the scene before the darkness is absolute, so she runs quickly. She runs *as if* she were fleeing, like the actor staging his own flight. Theatrical fugitive. From that city. From that teenager. She breaks away from all that. The gravity: a foot: the anti-gravity: a foot: the air running out. Where did she learn all this? The breathing: a stampede of horses. Something wild or something on the verge of death. A silent stampede: a noise felt more in the gesture that causes it than in the sound where it takes shelter. The cry. That city. That teenager.

When she arrives at the scene of the first crime, still under the weak evening light, she doesn't find anything unusual. She checks the trash accumulating in small irregular piles, prowls with slow curiosity around the corner, runs her fingers over the crumbling bricks: a poem under her fingertips. Can a poem be a trap? She sees what she saw: the body and its angles and the blood. She remakes it with millimetric precision in her memory, that, what she saw. Then, like her shadow, the unseen also appears. Did two people come to read this poem in the brick? Can an invitation become a challenge? Did two people walk a short distance to kneel here, before these words? Did they celebrate the discovery? Did they kiss while one or the other pushed the blade against his sex? Can poetry also end this way? The Detective crouches first and then, squatting, reaches out an arm to touch the little pebbles of the asphalt. The birds again, their flight.

"I am your spectator," she hisses through her teeth to the sky. "I'm here, looking at what you wanted me to see." She stands up.

She slaps the sides of her body with her open palms. About to leave, she pauses. She looks at the scene again.

"You have an audience now," she quietly repeats. The resentment. The impotence. "Come out," she hisses with her jaw clenched. "Come out, I'm dying to applaud you."

# 36

## The Tribute

His beauty surprises her. Male beauty always does that, surprises her. As if she never expected it. As if it were always happening for the first time. She studies the face in the photograph the Weeping Woman holds in her left hand and the only thing she says, literally, is: but what a beautiful man! A buried exclamation. It's about victim number Two. Fair skin. Black eyes. Librarian. It's about a private, embarrassed silence: the gaze scrabbling for something nonexistent on the ground. The tip of a shoe. It's about the obscene trajectory that leads to the violent death, tracing what life has sensually left behind on albumen paper.

"He was a normal man," the Woman with whom the Librarian had shared the last months of his life assures her. "His books. His routine. His house. A couple of friends. Nothing extraordinary. Nothing eccentric."

The Detective remembers his hands, man number Two's hands. Soft, certainly. So silky they seemed not to have lifelines, fingerprints, markers of identity. His eccentric hands, she thinks, remembering them as she saw them: lifeless on the mortuary bed. Orphans. The hands that, despite the taboo or disgust or fear, she had grazed with her own hands.

"But you didn't live together, did you?"

"What are you trying to say?" she answers defensively, wiping away her tears. "Are you implying I didn't know him well?"

"I'm not implying anything," she tells her quietly, trying to mask the annoyance she feels, a sort of exasperation. "I'm just saying that you didn't live together, or at least that he had an apartment in another building. Right?"

She nods. She looks at the Detective, then turns away.

"He never wanted to let go of that apartment. He spent some nights there." She pauses, hesitates, finally turns around. "Quite a few nights."

"He lived there, really," murmurs the Detective, looking down, "and he spent some nights here."

The woman's crying irritates her. She looks at her tears and the hand that passes over her cheek, laying waste to them, and she can't feel compassion for her. There's something there, in how she grieves, that corresponds not to the death of the man but to herself. The Weeping Woman weeps for the woman abandoned in a lonely apartment, the single woman, the husbandless woman. The Weeping Woman doesn't weep for him, for the man she saw stretched out on the mortuary slab. The man she admired even in death and who, even dead, she touched. The Weeping Woman can't see past her own nose, she can't get out of Herself.

"But he did have a special interest in contemporary art," says the Detective, trying to steer the conversation elsewhere. "You mentioned that in our first interview, didn't you?"

"A purely informal interest," the Weeping Woman assures her. "He never wrote anything about it. It was a sort of hobby. Something he did without me. Anyway, his true passion was books."

"Without you?" Her sudden incorporation into the discussion of a dead man forces her to pay attention.

"I never liked any of that," confirms the Librarian's ex-Girlfriend as she looks at her directly, her eyes coated in dried tears. Gone tears. Nonexistent tears. "I didn't understand it. It irritated me, actually. You don't have to share all your partner's interests," she asserts after a brief vacillation. An apology. A justification.

"True," murmurs the Detective. "You don't have to."

When she gets into her car, she repeats the phrase: you don't have to. She looks at the traffic lights, the store windows, the sky. There's bird shit on her windshield. She turns on the radio. You don't have to. A love song. The state of the weather. The traffic. The gas. Two clouds. Three. When she repeats the phrase to her Assistant on speakerphone, she does so slowly, without further explanation.

"That's what she said?"

"That," she confirms. "Exactly that."

"The forgotten girl? The fear of the death of love? The solitary woman in the desert?"

"Even angrier," she says and thinks at the same time. "More in the tenor of *the cold will pay. And the thunder.*"

"The tribute," he interrupts.

"That."

---

# 37

# Sensations of Exodus

Outside: the night: inside.

The lamp light, on.

The book containing Alejandra Pizarnik's diaries: on the right-hand side of the bed, on the wooden floor. A yellow pencil between its pages.

The Detective's eyes, closed.

A sword (flaming) (svelte) (metaphysical) in her hands.

# 38

## In a Field, and with the Help of Two Mirrors, I Buried a Sunbeam in the Earth

She notes: To allow the danger to aim at me. To place myself in the blankness of the now. To put the world in a here and now from which I cannot escape.

Then she sees her.

She sees me.

She acknowledges my approach. What will she flee from? she wonders as she watches me run from the other side of the window. The gravity. Lack of gravity. A woman in a hurry. Always. If we weren't about to talk about Gina Pane, I might even smile at her.

"Before anything else, you should know they died a while ago," I manage to tell her between gasps, right after glancing at the open book that covers almost the entire surface of the table. I say it right before chugging a bottle of water.

"I know," the Detective answers, staring with the intentness of someone trying in vain to recognize me.

*24 April 1963*

*To see a face exactly as it is. Impossible, if one of my glances vanishes as soon as I look with excessive intensity. Put an-other way: as if my eyes were enemies intent on interfering:*

*the absent eye deforms and transforms what the faithful wit-
ness gathers, the present eye.*

"Evidently the message writer likes knives," she says, handing
me the text with Message No. 6 from the Traveler with an Emptied Glass. We look each other in the eye. Dubious. Wary. Conspiratorial. How long ago? How long? How? A paper bridge. A
bridge made of text.

"But there are other artists, many more, aren't there?" she asks
aloud, looking at me as if she'd known me her whole life. "Why
Pane? Why not another woman? Another man?"

The smile of the purest irony. The smile of resignation.

"That, my dear Detective, is something you should investigate,
not me." The challenge falls naturally from my lips. A nuclear
flower. A provocation. How long?

*31 May 1962*

*Memories from childhood: walls, detonations, screams. The
air is a concentration camp for a tiny girl dancing on the
edge of a knife.*

"The body. The pain. The wound. Perhaps because of the opening that every wound is. A mark. An entrance, too. The light at the
end of the tunnel," she lists with almost scientific slowness. "My
body is an instrument of pain, she seems to say," she says.

"For all those reasons, yes, clearly," I stammer. "That must be
why she was chosen, for that and for the sunbeam they've buried,
don't you think?"

*28 July 1962*

*Sometimes it's the thirst, sometimes the cry of a timeless
abandonment. Sometimes I cry in my thirst, I cry through*

*my thirst, because sometimes my thirst is my communion,*
*my way of living, of witnessing my birth, of liberating myself*
*and taking a leap of faith. But sometimes I cry remotely for*
*the other that I am, the fugitive in my blood, the deluded, the*
*adventurer who left in the night to chase the sad faces their*
*sick desire flashed before them.*

"Because of the lyricism of the action? the outdated romanticism? the terrible illusion? the pathetic child's play? the summer stitch?" The questions now as slow as the list before it. Shots that eventually hit the target.

Here.

Now.

"'Noon on July 20, 1969, in Eco, France,'" she reads and cuts herself off. "A stitch," she adds.

In the photograph: the thin, almost androgynous body of a woman with short blond hair. Brown pants, the collar sky blue. An enormous round watch on her left wrist. The earth like earth. A minute mirror in each hand and in the middle of the black hole, at the back of the dark cave, at the entrance to a tunnel that doesn't yet exist, that rectangle of light. Something primeval.

## IN A FIELD, AND WITH THE HELP OF TWO MIRRORS, I BURIED A SUNBEAM IN THE EARTH

*2 January 1963*

*You are not at fault for your poem speaking about what it*
*is not. If it speaks about what it is, it means that someone*
*did not come instead of coming. But why do I speak with*
*active verbs as if I had spent the night with a sword in my*
*hand?*

"And no one ever dug it up?" she asks.

Someone isn't there. Someone has left. The Detective is a woman who flees.

"You're thinking about something else," I calmly contend, proceeding almost immediately to scrutinize her. I scrutinize her gaze. I drink some water.

She responds: *Sensations of exodus.*

She responds: *Fear of winter. Fear that it will go away.*

She responds: *Breath like suffocation.*

She responds: *No one wants to be scenery.*

Loose phrases. Scraps. Truncated pieces. Stolen words. Texts. Graphic robberies.

"But in the landscape now there's a hole and at the bottom of the hole is a rectangle of light that no one sees, that no one will see," I say, and I scrutinize her. I scrutinize her gaze. I drink some water.

"I spent the night with a sword in my hand," she says, definitively elsewhere. Gone.

"You're doing it all wrong. Come," I say, concerned. I take her by the hand, and as if she were convalescing, suffering a terminal illness, I lead her out of the restaurant. Into the city of the Castrated Men. An alley.

The path is very long. The path is so long that it seems to lead us into the center of the earth. The path is the center of the earth.

"Here." I point to it. It's a promontory. A little mountain of loose dirt, cement, and trash. An urban island that's really a sudden inner shore.

"Here," I repeat. "Here and now."

"Good."


Hands in the earth. Nails full of earth. The mouth. The nose. The breath. Everything in the earth.

## 39

---

# It Took Its Toll, *the Abandonment*
# *He Confined Me To*

I don't want to talk about him.
It doesn't interest me.
It had been years since I'd seen him.
It took its toll, the abandonment he confined me to.
Unforgivable. Unshakable. Irreversible.
That's how he should have behaved.

I don't want to talk about my son.
I don't want to.

I have a dead son. That's all.
But he was already dead.

(From the visit to victim number Three's father.)

# 40

## It Has to Fall, Eventually

The right shoe on the floor. The left shoe. The gust of wind that makes you close your eyes, pull up the neck of your shirt, stuff your hands in your pockets. The stooped body. The thought: this is the sad brown color of dusty days. The idea of finding yourself in the middle of a dune, in another country, being another person. The Detective looks up; there are kites in the sky, and then she glances unenthusiastically to the edge of the square, to the row of stone benches where no one ever sits. One of them should be occupied by a waiting journalist who, and she has insisted on this, really is a journalist. The wind distracts her. The wind demands she look up: If only she could breathe or rest or something. Something else. Anything else. She's about to smile.

"Do you want to try?" The voice catches her by surprise, the whisper. In front of her, just a few steps away, is someone she hadn't seen, she hadn't been able to see through the dust, the pollution. She almost runs into him. She almost kisses him: that sensation.

"You like it, don't you?" presses the old man, offering her the end of a string that climbs toward the sky and culminates in a rhomboidal construction.

"What is it?" she asks, pointing at the kite.

"My favorite dragon."

The Detective studies him, the dragon. Slowly. The dust on her molars. That taste. Distrust. Someone is there, on the bench. A journalist, waiting for her. The agitated air, smelling of salt, gas, combustion. The dust. Then, without thinking about it, she takes the string the man holds out to her. The soft pressure of the air. The sensation of being connected to something invisible and superior. The smile now widens. The security of being, in this moment, the girl she never was.

"Like that," the man tells her, pulling the thread and brushing her shoulder, her forearm with his bony hand, his old-man hand. "The idea," he murmurs, "is to get the dragon soaring overhead. Remaining there."

The urgency, now, that the great beyond is the color blue. Sky blue. If she could be on a dune, being someone else.

"But it has to fall, eventually," she answers, still looking up. "It has to come back eventually, doesn't it?"

"Ah, miss," the man exclaims as he shakes his head. Then he snatches the string and turns away from her without another word.

She's alone in the middle of an enormous square, lambasted by gusts of wind that impede her step, her vision, and she doesn't know, doesn't really know, if she's held the string in her hands, if she's talked to an old man, if a dragon has connected her to a beyond of another color. From afar, at the edge of the square that looks like a continent, an infinite dune, there should be someone waiting for her. There. A woman on a bench. That she knows. There's a journalist who wants to talk to her about Alejandra Pizarnik. But she doesn't know if she wants to, if she herself wants to talk today, in a square with the strange dimensions of a continent full of dunes, about a poet who seems to be a madman's obsession. Not today.

---

# 41

## Penis Envy

Mark Seltzer is a scholar of crime, someone who believes there is a link between the violent acts (repetitive, mechanical, compulsive) of a serial killer and the styles of production and reproduction in machine culture. Serial killers, who kill and cut and roam free, literalize, Seltzer believes, the principles of contemporary posthuman production. A serial killer is a cutting machine. A gullible man.

But a serial killer, Seltzer says, is also fascinated with the wound. He's someone who wants to look inside.

"Inside?" Valerio repeats, emphasizing one of the terms he hears her speak aloud as she reads the text.

"Yes, inside, inside a body," clarifies the Detective, barely looking up from the page but maintaining a silence typical when waiting for something else.

"As if the penis were the key to a door," the Assistant continues, suddenly inspired. "As if they were getting rid of the lock on the door so they could sniff around at leisure."

"Metaphorically, clearly," the Detective interrupts him. Dubitatively. Unexpectedly smooth.

"Metaphorically, of course," he says. "At leisure."

Then they look at each other again. Their eyes meet. As if the eye were the key to a body. As if they truly wanted to know what was happening inside.

"Who would want a penis, Valerio? Who'd want to put a penis somewhere else?"

The Assistant clears his throat before answering:

"Someone who doesn't have a penis, of course," he says. His voice tremulous. "Someone who wants to have a penis."

"You don't mean the famous envy, do you?" the Detective says as she looks up at the ceiling laced with cracks; she theatrically turns her back on him.

"Perhaps I mean the envy that isn't so famous," Valerio murmurs, his voice growing quieter. "The envy of the penis itself, for example."

"A penis that wants a penis? Is that what you're trying to say? That a penis wants a penis?"

"Why not? A man, for example. A cuckolded man. A man who's been left for someone else. A penis for another penis."

"A man who's been turned into a woman, is that what you're saying?"

"A man who wants to recover something that's his," he concludes.

She looks at him again. She thinks serial killers' minds are incredibly boring. She meets his gaze. Suddenly the sensation that the eye is indeed the key to the body. Suddenly the curiosity.

# 42

---

## An Area Enclosed by a Circle

Think about what an expert in serial killers must think about when they feel wet, open, scandalous lips on their own mouth. Think about the word "literalize" when a hand full of fingers advances— a legion of ants—toward the southern part of their pubis. Think about the phrase "cutting engine" when they open their two legs and close them: scissors: gadgets: brandished blades. Then, along with the trembling breath that grows and throngs, come the echoes of their words. Think about the sword.

*Sex: the only place where everything is permitted.*

It's a berth: the feminine bed. Bedding that hasn't been washed in three weeks. Open books, one by Alejandra Pizarnik. Unsharpened pencils on the nightstand. Socks under pillows. Too heavy a comforter (comfort-her? for her comfort?). It's a lamp turned on. A green wall: aquamarine: aqua. And the nakedness (wasn't it *death's business* to strip?): a man and a woman. Their bones. Their skin: the body's largest organ. Their pubic hair: amber. Their freckles. Their fingernails: chewed. Their touch. Their sudden urgency. Their imbrication. It's the truth.

*The sexual act: a sort of area enclosed by a circle.*

It's the truth: the only one that exists. For her comfort. The surroundings: in flight. The sensation of being inside the fishbowl the pulse has become. Bam. Boom. Bam. The utter concentration of the touch. Fingerprints like microscopes. The mental absence. The presence: entire. A shoulder. An elbow. A knee. The teeth: biting. The hair entangled with saliva. The saliva entangled with the ear. The ear entangled with the tongue. The tongue, ah, the smell. The smell's punch. The smell's sword. The smell of the plural body: a bouquet of members tied together with a silk ribbon. A concatenation. The smell and then, simultaneously, the taste. The complexity of the taste.

You taste, he's heard saying, like yellow (wheat) (chamomile) (tree).

You taste, she's heard saying, like green (citrus) (summer) (flowing water) (pear).

It's a berth. They're two bodies. It's a bitter taste of not knowing. And the way they have of listening to each other: a sigh dissolving in the air. Learning to shudder. Air diluting in the nostril. Cocaine. Communion wafer. The tiniest touch: the underside (and the backside) of the sex.

*You can make love with anyone. It's like going to the cinema:*

And to see. To see what the eyes see when they don't see anything. To see another world from another world: to cease seeing. To see the unknown and, within the unknown, to see the unknown, too. To say his name: To Say: Valerio. And to unknow him, indeed. In that very moment. His body in hers and around it. To Say: Valerio. To say: you also taste like red. This color. The index finger across the sheet, the idiotic smile on the face.

*It's like going to the cinema: a silence and a participation.*

Their laughter. The color red on their thighs, at the corners of their mouths, under their nails. To say: we won't have children. To say: without a doubt. The laughter and the explosion of the laughter and the echo of the explosion of the laughter that, along their bodies, forms a circular wall protecting the sex. Crepuscular red. Fire red. Menstruation red. Final burning red.

*Afterward you smoke and you talk and you argue.*

January 4, Friday, 1963.

Then, while he sleeps (face-up) (magazine model) (man tinged with abstract red) she thinks (she looks at him and thinks) that someone, one of the two, has committed a murder. Everything gives them away: The color gives them away. The positions of their bodies give them away. The silence gives them away. Then she wonders, she can't help it: Why isn't he afraid? Why is he not afraid? In the time that precedes pleasure and the time following it, the man hasn't felt any fear. He's in an unknown house, in an unknown bed, in an unknown body, and not for a second, not for even the tiniest sliver of that second, has he let himself be interrupted by fear. Or doubt. Or suspicion. In his world, in the world of To Say: Valerio, that doesn't exist. And perhaps it's that or perhaps it's habit that makes her fling her hand toward the other skin (the body's largest organ) and stop, as before a screen, to repeat: this is the scene of a crime. This is.

# 43

## The Fetus of a Woman in the Belly of a Bed

The nightmare wakes her. A moan. An arm's sudden movement. The images fleeing, terrified, in the presence of light. An echo. Before getting out of bed, before placing her bare feet on the floorboards and looking out at the sunlight, the Detective curls up on her right side and pulls the blankets to cover her face, her body. A fetus, that's it. The fetus of a woman in the belly of a bed. That's what she is. A question: Who exonerates? Two questions: Who exonerates the exonerator? Who relieves? Three questions: Who dies again and again and then again? Is that what exempts? Who deserves punishment? Four questions: Who dares to say: "I am not the murderer"? Will you alleviate me? What does the exonerator exonerate? Who flees the scene of their own crime? Five questions: Do I want to find you, murderer? Will I want to see my face in yours? Who pardons? Who rests? Who dares to say: "I am not you"? Six questions: Who buries? What does the exonerator's saliva taste like when the relatives weep? Who kills? Who dictates the punishment and who metes it out? Who wants to see the face of the person who has killed on TV? Who erases? Seven questions: But who truly kills? And who dies again and again and then over and over again? What does the exonerator see when they look at the entrance orifice and the bullet casing and the exit orifice? Who exempts? Who bears the weight of the dead on their shoulders in their eyes their hands their nails their lips? Who closes their eyes? Who opens them?

The morning silence.

# 44

## Valerio's Report

This is how Valerio's report should be written:

1) You have split ends. And even though your apartment door may look open, there is a sort of transparent, gummy film, a sort of spiderweb made of cellophane, stuck to the furniture and the objects and the floors and the walls, making everything untouchable. No one can touch anything in your house, Detective. No one can run their fingertips, with all their fingerprints, their history, their horrors, their identity, over the actual surface. No one can touch you.

2) The accent; your accent. I hadn't noticed it. Not until you talked half asleep, or not completely awake, toward the edge of the morning. A strange accent. Unrecognizable, yes, but present. To Say: Valerio. And to say it like that and not another way, a way that suggests: I come from far away and I am not here. I will never be all here. Because that is, at the end of the day, the weight of an accent, isn't it? The weight of an accent that only emerges, when it emerges, on the shores of sleep. On the shores of wakefulness.

3) And the scream, yours, the softer one. The scream disguised as a moan that brings you back from a nightmare.

Because it was a nightmare, wasn't it? I'm sure it was a nightmare. And the words, if you're interested, if you don't already know, were: Shoot. Bullet. Man. Dead. Night. I imagine you were dreaming about the case that consumes your hours and minutes and seconds. I imagine you were trying to escape, to leave, to put everything aside. I'll always remember that scream, I know. And those eyes of yours, the gaze of the criminal or the unhinged, facing the circle of light that marks them as the culprit. As the sole culprit. Your lost eyes, Detective; and your scream, the softer one.

4) Your feet: shockingly soft. No one would think at the sight of them that you like to walk. That you walk so much.

5) The bachelor's mess in your room: sudden identification. Total recognition. You are me: I am you. Biunivocal.

5a) Can a man really be a woman and vice versa?

6) And I was there, and when I woke up, it was as if I never was. Because no one can truly be (which is another way of saying touch) (which is another way of saying mark inscribe engrave) in a place (which is another way of saying your body) so protected (or so desolated) by layers and more layers of that invisible yet real substance (which is another way of saying glue).

7) You talk to yourself. You talk at night. You talk to the window. You talk too much.

8) And what will I do now, after I've seen you where the natural light of the sun never shines? Will I lower my eyes like a reprimanded schoolchild or will I look at you, as I always have, with the from-afar-ness that you impose, even from this closeness, on everything around you? Will I have the same voice, and will I speak in that same voice to say "good morning" and later "good afternoon" and even later "sleep well"? Will I walk by your side and hand you papers and

will I pass you the phone like when I walked by your side and handed you papers and passed you the phone? And how will I look at your hand that's touched me? And your tongue that's tasted me? And your cheek that rested on my right shoulder? There, outside, in the world, at the end or beginning of the day, will I remember anything?

And it goes without saying that Valerio's report (which is just another way of saying To Say: Valerio) would never be written like this. There simply would be no way.

# 45

## Male Friendships

She asks about him, his twenty-seven-year-old friend, dark, brown-eyed. She asks carefully, her gaze fixed on the ground, attempting to avoid those eyes of his where a crack, an empty point, now opens up. An amputation. She says to him: your information will be crucial. She also tells him that her hopes, if she still has any, if they even exist, are on him. The fourth victim's friend looks a lot like the fourth victim (the Detective can't stop thinking about this): a teacher (like him), 1.69 meters tall (like him), another normal man (like him).

They're outside the circle of bodies: they're inside the language: that kind of sociality. They drink coffee. They place their nervous hands on the table: unexpected little doves. Alabaster objects. The noise of raucous students amid all that.

Saying: I told him to be careful.

Saying: *He was always afraid of winter. Afraid it would go away.*

Saying: He didn't want to see that whole show, especially after their encounters last year. I know he forced himself to go. He'd thought about it all day while crossing the city (I'm almost certain), in the same way he thought about Abramović's work since he'd heard of it. He almost went back. He almost decided not to go in.

But once inside, he occupied himself with some texts in the entrance to the gallery: don't interfere with the danger, avoid it, in fact, contain it. And he wondered (I'm almost certain) if he could receive it. Confront it. He needed a place to be there without being noticed, not too close, not too much in the middle, not too far. He focused on the row of knives and the surprising beauty of the scenography. Like many early modernists, Abramović confronted him directly (I'm almost certain) instead of letting him look and judge as art of the past often does. Like the minimalists, she transformed the scenography into a place, making it his place, too. And like much introspective art, she forced him to confront himself and to feel somewhat ashamed (I'm almost certain) for doing so. By the gallery's standards, people stayed for a long time, not even daring to smile, speak, or move. Some came back again and again. Some never had the guts to return. Some couldn't resist the telescope, others ran away. It's easy to understand the strange mix of motives for being there: the guilt of treating famine like just another spectacle, morbid fascination, genuine appreciation for the work. Only later and very slowly could she capture the public's attention and, having done so, absorb them completely (I'm almost certain). She stood in the middle for a long time, almost expressionless. Erect despite everything, or kneeling with utter precariousness on the step, she drew closer to the audience and the danger, then drew them closer to each other. Through the telescope, with astonishing precision, her somber expression almost dissolved in her eyes and in her overly soft skin, if you consider everything she's endured. I'm almost certain of all of this. Although, in any case, it's common knowledge that a low-calorie diet can keep a person looking young.

Saying: I'm almost certain that show was important.

And he fixes his eyes on the Detective's eyes as if he's just revealed the solution to a great mystery, now totally decoded. His mystery.

Days later (after walking again and again through the Alley of the
Castrated Man) (after returning to work and leaving work) (after
remembering again and again, again and again, again and again,
the crime scenes) (after being prompted To Say: Valerio) (after
eating and forgetting to eat and eating forgetting everything)
(after finding the book in the tangled sheets of her bed) (after
going to the movies and seeing a film she doesn't remember) (after
listening to the music that, according to Valerio's report, the other
suspect listens to) (after showering and not showering) (after
drinking her morning coffee and her evening beer) (after everything referred to as daily life that occurs, generally, between pa-
rentheses), the Detective will remember that look.

She will return to it, the look, as if it were a place. She will return to it, the look that's really a place but hidden from itself. Only
she will realize she's there (the oasis) (the enigma) (the eureka)
(the floating desert) when she is there. The gaze of the friend of
victim number Four. Has anyone ever had a gaze like that? Does
that exist?

Saying: He seemed distraught after that show (the inquisitive
gaze). As if he'd left as one person and returned as another (his
eyes embarrassed by the cliché). I had a hard time recognizing
him (the shrugging shoulders). I could barely talk to him (the
straining lips).

Saying: But I always told him to be careful.

Saying: Of what?

Saying: Well of himself, who else?

Days later, just after she's rounded a corner, the Detective will
wonder, insistently, about the violence in which male friendships
are forged.

# 46

## No Talent Whatsoever

Someone knocks on the door. From behind the door, someone says they need to talk to me. It's nighttime. Before saying anything, I peer out the window and confirm Valerio is still there: the faint light of a lit cigarette inside a car. Obstinate firefly. The wind that lays waste to nocturnal nothings. The trembling leaves. I question it while I go to the kitchen for the key, and as I turn the key in the lock, I still question it. It's her voice, the Detective's voice. An entrance orifice. Her voice with no way out.

"I've been reading Alejandra Pizarnik," she says by way of greeting as soon as I open the door. "I want to talk about her," she presses, flipping through the book in her hand. "I want to understand."

As I turn to peek at the kitchen clock, I wonder how many minutes it will take to regret what I'm now doing: greeting her, inviting her in, offering her tea, water, whiskey. When she swiftly opts for the third, I'm already sorry. That's when she falls onto the sofa. Her boots resting on the floorboards. The weight.

"Long day?" I ask. Manners.

"The longest," she answers as she accepts the glass, not looking up from the book she's placed on the table. "What I don't understand, Professor," she begins without preamble after the first sip, clearing her throat, "is why or how a mere bipolar nymphomaniac has been able to con so many poetry lovers."

Her gaze, clear. Direct. The angular mouth. A party. She's caught me off guard, it's true. The smell of sweat. The stench of cocaine. I wasn't expecting it, which is why I do something else I didn't expect: pour myself a whiskey. Two ice cubes. I watch her. I don't want to answer. I want to remain impartial and neutral. I want, definitely, to have another voice.

"The case is getting complicated for you, isn't it?" When I raise my glass and offer it to her—a toast—I realize I've fallen just as deeply as she has, I'm falling. "It must be difficult," I continue. "It must be very difficult to read the news these days. The headlines. Difficult for you."

"People like you," she retorts. "People like you spend years reading poets like this. Identification? Desire? Envy? Suicidal urges? Lack of talent? Urges to kill?"

As the list of her questions grows, I wonder, peeking at the kitchen clock, why her need to know feels like pricks on my shoulder. Knives against my skin. Halfhearted slaps. I wonder when she'll back out. It's the gaze I know: vertical in the process of ascension. For a moment I get the sense that the Detective believes she's immortal. The image: there is a woman sunk into my living room couch. The shapeless mass. The ancestral weight.

"It must be horrible, chasing a devil," I tell her conciliatorily. "It must be even worse to find him," I whisper, gesturing to the book with the almost-emptied glass. An oblique smile on my face. One page.

"When I was a girl," she recalls, "I saw the dwarf tightrope-walker with the sack of bones." She too points to the book. "I saw her," she insists, looking out from places unfamiliar to me. That sort of distance or rancor. There's a city beyond her pupils, a neighborhood she's still trying to escape. There's a window she stands behind to develop, peacefully and warmly, the life she doesn't have. The life that looks and, looking at her, escapes her. The Detective walks down the Alley of the Castrated Man with her fists clenched and the sound of molars in vertical tension, trying to fit together. The imperfection of a set of teeth. The indents of fingernails on her palms.

"This wouldn't be so bad except that it is," she says. And then, still looking at me from that personal hiding place, she falls quiet.

"Except that it is," I tell her, meddling in a game that feels macabre from here.

"It's just that it isn't," she repeats, "or would be or is."

Something happens in the world. Something must be happening, something like a gust of wind, something without a solution, for the Detective to stand before me, motionless: a dry-lipped automaton, a wide-eyed reciter, a dwarf on a tightrope.

"Reading," I whisper later, much later, "shouldn't be so complicated. A matter of turning the page."

The taste of the whiskey makes me close my eyes, and behind my eyelids, I see you. You must know how to whistle: you have that kind of mouth. Where's my blood? you ask. All this is a cemetery, I tell you. This is the Kingdom of the Here.

"I suppose you believe the murderer or murderess is smarter than me," she states without looking away from me, automaton. "I suppose you believe they're more talented than me."

The taste of the whiskey makes me close my eyes, and there is no longer anyone behind my eyelids.

"Judging by the newspapers, my dear," I answer, "your issue is more a question of not having any talent. No talent whatsoever."

She smiles. She pouts her lips. She cocks her head. She straightens it again, her head. She looks at me with the widest eyes opened even wider. She rests her elbows on her parted knees. She has crossed the glass. She stands up. She is a back that retreats.

Once she closes the door behind her (the bang, an unusual silence), I know all I have to do now is wait. Sooner or later, I'll know what the Detective is capable of.

# 47

## It's Like Being Swallowed by a Dead Man

She stops. It happens suddenly, with no premeditation. It's brought about: instead of continuing down the narrow hallway where the sun's natural light never reaches, the Detective remains still. More like: the Detective is suspended. A few typewritten pages in her hands. Blue pants. Blue blouse. A button split in two. Lips parted. Eyeglasses. Breath. In that instant she hears everything, she sees everything, she smells everything, she touches everything. She feels everything. Beneath her feet, the green tiles laid there by someone years ago, decades ago even, without thinking about the moment, this moment occurring so long after, when her feet will transmit the precise information: green tiles under my feet. The air: wispy, thin, barely breathable. The light: so little, so scarce, so artificial. The truly yellow light. The light everyone calls electric. The sound, now, of the electricity. That soft humming. That moan. The speed of the people who move down the hallway without noticing the fact that they are people hurriedly moving down a hallway. The face, now indifferent, of a man who stops before her and utters words. Orders. Instructions. You have to do this. You have to do that. ("You have to put an end to this right now": she makes out that phrase, its echoes. "I need you on other business. Got it?") The body of the other young man who emanates a scent she struggles to name and that, nevertheless, she knows. And later she recognizes all this with utmost ease, almost at once. The scent of the sweat and the morning coffee and the sweetness that sometimes breaks off from bread and the grimy newspaper and the glass of the cup she has drunk water from. The scent, too, of the drunk water. Cool, ingested water. The scent of the morning rush and the brushing together of bodies on buses and subways and of the desire when frustrated, when it does nothing but produce its own protocol. Her own. The scent. Ah. The scent of the visited body. The weary sound (syncopated music) (something without rhythm) of people together: their steps, their voices, their emotions. The faces, the multiple faces reflected in the window: their monstrous faces, their human faces, their suddenly unfamiliar faces. (Got it?) The internal voyage of blood (that sound), the incessant drumming of the pulse (that sound), the subtle scratching of the breath (that sound). And that sensation, the nameless sensation that forces her to bring her hand to her stomach and leave it there, tremulous, while she waits for the suspended moment to pass or change or end entirely while she is overwhelmed by the nausea, the doubt, the confirmation: It's like being swallowed by a dead man.

*Alejandra: it has been forty days of unspeakable anguish. Forty days of muffled loneliness.*
*Alejandra: you have to fight terribly.*

The memory of the words. Surprising in their precision. Accurate.

# 48

## What She Shouldn't

"When life becomes nothing but a nightmare," she murmurs between swigs of beer, "I start to think you're the prime suspect in this case."

She says it, immediately letting out a gentle, astonishingly silent laugh. She says it and, immediately incredulous, takes it back. She looks at me. She thinks she looks at me. She imagines she looks at me. The laughter is a grimace. The laughter and the echo of the laughter fade away, chasing after each other amid the noise of the place. Electronica music. Among the gesticulation of the place. A circus. An instantaneous insane asylum. She says it and the person she imagines I am can do nothing but listen to her like when you listen to an echo chasing after the sound of a voice in a crowded place. The very incredulity of the woman imagined by the Detective makes her shut out the noise. *The one I used to be* is here, *along my peripheral vision.* And it's a vision that's almost drunk, blurry, in flight. The vision of a woman who hasn't slept. The vision of a woman who thinks.

"You can't make head nor tail of this one," she says. She says it sorrowfully, and then, weighed down with defeat, she shrugs. She shouldn't say that. Do that. She shouldn't be here, talking to herself, drinking beer (the bitterness of the beer, the coldness of the beer), moving her hips subtly, oh so subtly. She shouldn't talk non-sense. Split in two. Open up. She shouldn't imagine things. She shouldn't, above all, imagine suspects. She shouldn't lean forward, with utmost delicacy, over the glass shelf where the line of coke extends, perfectly straight. She shouldn't snort it with that half pleasure and half guilt that compels her back to the dance floor, to lose herself among the crowd. She shouldn't. The subtle hips. The oscillating movement. The burning gaze. She shouldn't reach her arms up or close her eyes or spin on her own axis. A fifteen-year-old girl. A lost teenager. An outcast. Patches on the knees of her blue pants. She shouldn't let in the repetitive, caustic sound that then slides slowly, so slowly, through the long veins of her body and tickles her later, much later, on the soles of her feet. The rhythm. The beating of her heart. The sweat. She shouldn't move, keep moving. She shouldn't look at the young man as if he were the approximately thirty-year-old Young Man found lifeless in an alley of the city. Lamentable, the events. Brutal, the homicide. A cannibal, the thief. She shouldn't imagine sparkling headlines or draft long news articles full of graphic details for the tabloid she publishes with strict regularity inside her own head. She shouldn't be her own best reader. The only one. She shouldn't approach. She shouldn't move away.

"This one does have a head, what he doesn't have are genitals, don't you think?" And she shouldn't ask this question of the person who isn't me but who dances with her on that dance floor that seems, under the flashing lights, to be full of body parts. Fragments of bodies. Pieces of bodies.

On the dance floor there's a woman who dances; a woman who likes to dance.

She shouldn't open her eyes again, surprised. Or see what she sees. See what she just said. See her own words on a giant screen framed with blue neon lights. YOU CAN'T MAKE HEAD NOR

TAIL OF THIS ONE. She shouldn't look at the big letters or start laughing again. No. No, she shouldn't lean on that shoulder, a shoulder, signaling, with the tip of her index finger, the words she imagines all by herself.

"This one really does have a head, but what he doesn't have are genitals, you know?" She definitely shouldn't say that. This. She shouldn't repeat it. Nor should she maintain a sudden, solemn silence then flooded, without warning, by the deafening noise of the voices and the synthesizers and the bodies before she explodes into that laughter of hers, so silent, so crooked, a mockery of itself, a weapon against itself, a wound against itself. None of that should happen. None of that should be happening. Not even I, moving in sync with her movement thanks to her imagination, shadow of her shadow, hand of her hand, should explode, as if I'd been waiting beside her my whole life for this opportunity. I shouldn't double over in laughter or gently lean my torso toward her or wrap my arm around her left shoulder. Fugitives. Shameless. Fired up. Nor should she again let out that fierce, silent, defeated laughter, because all that, all this, this movement, oh so subtle, in the drunken crowd, this sensation of producing your own theory of hell, your own experience of hell, all that, this, whatever it is, should not be. All this.

# 49

## Gargoyle in the Middle of the Square

What if one didn't know what month it was? What day? What time? There's a woman standing in the rain. A woman staring into the distance without moving a single muscle in her body. There's a woman sitting on the park bench. In the rain. In the persistence of the rain. And if one didn't know she was the Detective?

A gargoyle in the middle of a square. Stone thing. Fracture-matter.

I don't want to know anything about me (about you) (about her). I don't want to think. I don't want to look. I want to give up. To give. I want that. And to never know anything else about me (about her). Nothing about you (about me) (about him). I don't want to know about them.

What if I said something like that?

*I'm not from here. Never. I'm not from here. I'm leaving and I'm never coming back. No.*

I don't want to keep going. Not to continue. I don't want to run into the wall (the glass) (the teeth) again. I don't want this question. This other one. I don't want to know. I don't want to think. I don't want to show my face (buttocks) (thighs). I don't want the light of the flash. I don't want the face, that face, on the page. I don't want to see. I don't want to shoot.

What if I were saying something like that?

The rainwater makes her blouse transparent, her lips tremulous, the landscape incalculable. She isn't cold yet. She doesn't feel anything yet. This shouldn't happen.

*Apparently it is the end. I want to die. I want it seriously, with total vocation.*

Someone walks by on the other side of the window and looks in: the table set, the fire in the hearth, the glow of the home. The fleeing life. The guiltless life. Someone stops, surprised. Someone peers into Alejandra Pizarnik's eyes. A window. An abyss. The message is from the other side of the glass. This is not a laugh. Someone is watching us. Could Someone think that there, around that table? The message is untouchable. Someone hesitates when they see us fall silent, suddenly. The poetry. The message is beyond.

And this, too, shouldn't happen, of course.

# 50

## She Vehemently Claims

She tells her it's too late; that she's late, unfortunately.

"I'm not the one who missed the appointment," the Journalist responds, unable to hide her resentment. The Detective thinks that the woman before her looks unreal in the glare of the artificial light, more a cartoon than a human being. More a sketch than a woman. Perhaps that's why she looks at her and stops looking at her, intermittently. Letter-size sheets of paper in her hands. Wristwatch. People walking on the other side of the white wall. The gaze landing on all that.

"It isn't that," she starts to explain, then changes her mind. "So what did you want to talk to me about on that occasion?"

"About Pizarnik," she answers quickly. "About Alejandra Pizarnik."

"Ah, that." Her eyes again on the pages, on the watch, the real wall.

"She's the key, and you know it," she vehemently claims, "or you should know. You should. If you don't read her, if you don't read her closely, you'll never find the culprit."

The papers. The wristwatch. The white wall. The time.

"And who's interested in that, ma'am?" she asks, and immediately wonders if that really is her voice. If she's the one who's really saying what she hears herself say. Seldom the echo.

"Who's interested in what?"

"The culprit," she vehemently claims. "You heard me right."

"Well, you are," she exclaims, incredulous. "I am." Her eyes turn to tunnels, rage, secret passageways. "The dead men are. The dead men's survivors."

The Detective remembers the square, the wind in the square, the kite. That afternoon. There was a woman waiting on a bench. There was.

"The dead men," she tells her, "aren't interested in the culprit. They're interested in resting," she tells her. "The dead men's survivors," she tells her, "aren't interested in the culprit. They're interested in living," she tells her.

In the square, under the soaring kite, a girl who never was grips a string attached to it. The wind. A veil. The dust storm.

"But you are," insists the Journalist. "I am."

"You and I are what?"

"You and I are interested. We won't be able to live without this, without the culprit. We won't be able to die."

The Detective observes her, the kite, the cutting-stabbing object, the cut, the flight. Someone is running. Someone hasn't stopped running. The Detective looks at the bloody groin and the red puddle and the mother's gaze. A dust storm. Great feats. Someone getting away with it. The mockery. Then the Detective, barely thinking, takes the string. The gentle pressure of the wind. The feeling of being connected.

# IV

## The Longing for Prose

Dr. Cristina Rivera Garza
ITESM-Campus Toluca
[Submitted for review by the journal *Hispamérica;* its total
or partial reproduction is prohibited]

To write, from this perspective, amounts to inscribing a sign
on the surface of a dismembered body, or rather simply letting the tongue itself be carved up, become the voice of a
dissociated subject.[1]

—MARÍA NEGRONI

*Now*
*the young woman finds the mask of infinity*
*and cracks the wall of poetry.*[2]

—ALEJANDRA PIZARNIK,
translation by CECILIA ROSSI

---

1 Escribir, desde esta perspectiva, equivale a inscribir algún signo sobre la
superficie de un cuerpo desmembrado o bien, simplemente, a dejar que la
lengua misma se descuartice, se vuelva voz de un sujeto disociado.
2 Ahora
la muchacha halla la máscara del infinito
y rompe el muro de la poesía.

# 51

## The Prose of My Terrifying Language

### (INTROIT)

"What I desire is to write prose. Respect for prose, excessive re-spect for prose,"[1] Alejandra Pizarnik wrote in her diary on Sunday, June 21, 1964.[2] Penned by a poet who published *El árbol de Diana* (*Diana's Tree,* translated by Yvette Siegert) just two years earlier, a book with an original preface by Octavio Paz and which César Aira considers "a euclidean construction that transcends senti-mentalism without overshadowing the autobiographical im-pulse . . . [a book in which] the intensity has come to a head, the themes are decisive, the mechanism functions with a Mozart-like fluidity,"[3] this statement remains enigmatic.[4]

Ultimately, interest in the topic was hardly ephemeral. A cou-ple of years later, in 1966, she declared: "Deep, inenarrable (!) desire to write a little book in prose. I'm talking about an extremely

1 "Lo que yo deseo es escribir prosa. Respeto por la prosa, excesivo respeto por la prosa."
2 Alejandra Pizarnik, *Diarios,* ed. Ana Becciu, Barcelona, Lumen, 2003, 368. Translations mine, unless otherwise noted.
3 "Una construcción no euclidiana que trasciende el sentimentalismo sin anular el impulso autobiográfico . . . [un libro en el que] la intensidad ha cul-minado, los temas están decididos, el mecanismo funciona con una fluidez mozartiana."
4 César Aira, *Alejandra Pizarnik,* Barcelona, Omega, 2001, 55.

beautiful prose, about a really well-written book."[1] Later that year, Pizarnik insisted:

> I want to seriously study prose poetry. I don't understand why I chose this form. It imposed itself. Moreover, it has been in me since my first book. I've never read anything about it. . . .
>
> It's strange how obsessed I am with learning about prose poems, or perhaps, simply about prose. . . . Now, every day, the certainty of an impossible form of prose eats away at me.[2]

In 1967 she continued: "Increasingly I feel my strength is prose. Poem in prose or whatever in prose. I cannot versify in a strange, loathsome language. I want to indulge it in prose. Perfect prose—an impossible desire—whose outcome would be [*illegible*] the prose of my terrifying language."[3]

From one entry to the next, it is clear that in the final years of her life, which she ended by her own hand with a Seconal overdose in 1972, the Argentine poet Alejandra Pizarnik grew accustomed to returning repeatedly, and with growing fervor, to a topic that occupied much of her analytical and creative energy: the writing of prose. If *El árbol de Diana* was indeed the book with which

1 "Deseo hondo, inenarrable (!) de escribir en prosa un pequeño libro. Hablo de una prosa sumamente bella, de un libro muy bien escrito" (Pizarnik, *Diarios,* 412).
2 "Deseo estudiar muy seriamente el poema en prosa. No comprendo por qué elegí esa forma. Se impuso. Además, está en mí desde mi libro primero. Nunca leí nada al respecto. . . . Extraño es cómo y cuánto me obsesiona el aprendizaje de los poemas en prosa o tal vez, simplemente, de la prosa. . . . Ahora, cada día, me corroe la seguridad de una forma imposible de prosa" (Pizarnik, *Diarios,* 418).
3 "Cada vez más siento que lo mío es la prosa. Poema en prosa o lo que fuere en prosa. No puedo versificar en un lenguaje extraño y execrado. Quiero mimarlo en prosa. Prosa perfecta—imposible deseo—cuyo fin sería [*ilegible*] la prosa de mi idioma espantoso" (Pizarnik, *Diarios,* 434).

"you cannot go any further,"[1] Pizarnik decided to go further in *another way*. Instead of doing more of the same, and doing it better, the poet leapt with all her words "onto my prose like a fast train."[2] The simile here is by no means superfluous. Pizarnik refers to a leap as opposed to a transition, for instance. Moreover, she associates prose with a fast train: a vehicle in motion that can also become a source of danger when moving at top speed. Alejandra Pizarnik's relationship with prose, her longing for and through prose, was anything but simple.

Based on a close reading of her diaries and complete narrative writings, I propose to elucidate some of the threads entangled in the Pizarnikian longing for prose. I will read these texts in a deliberate attempt to avoid the romantic, stereotypical portrait of the suicidal poet obsessed with pain and death and instead explore the Pizarnik who, in her abundant and meticulous readings, dedicated herself to thinking—indeed, to thinking carefully and rigorously— about the limitations of poetry, as well as what she came to see, as her mental health deteriorated, as the refuge of prose. That home. I will read Alejandra Pizarnik's diaries because, as Ana Becciú states in her prologue introducing the volume she edited in 2003, "the writing of the diary is closely related to the search for a *prose,* the ambition to equip herself with a concrete language that would one day allow her to write a novel."[3]

Certainly, I am interested in her longing for prose. Yet I am also interested in the various ways she came to see this as a thwarted longing, albeit one wholly fulfilled, according to critics both then

1 "no se puede ir más lejos" (Aira, *Alejandra Pizarnik,* 55).
2 "para subir de un salto a mi prosa como un tren rápido" (Pizarnik, *Diarios,* 447).
3 "la escritura del diario está estrechamente relacionada con la búsqueda de una *prosa,* la ambición de dotarse de un lenguaje concreto que le permita un día escribir una novela" (Pizarnik, *Diarios,* 11).

and now. Because as much as her diary is filled with declarations of her interest in prose, it is also filled with accounts of its impossibility and even, as Pizarnik puts it, its failure. Though she cites many reasons, as could be expected, almost all of them end with and depart from that "terrifying language"[1] that, in her own words, makes up her own language and actions. What follows is an effort to identify, and bring to its logical conclusion, the terror of that language that troubles and produces the reality of Alejandra Pizarnik, prose writer.

1 "idioma espantoso"

# 52

## What Is She Talking About When She Talks About Prose?

### (FIRST CHAPTER)

It would suffice to flip through a few pages of *La bucanera de Pernambuco o Hilda la polígrafa* (*The Lady Buccaneer of Pernambuco or Hilda the Polygraph*), a text Pizarnik produced just a few years before her death and which was only published posthumously in 1982, to observe that this poet's ideas about prose were anything but conventional.[1] The text, which begins with two tables of content, one "naïve (or not),"[2] dedicated to Loth's daughters, and another "clever,"[3] dedicated to Fanny Hill's daughter, not only warns possible "readers" or "readeresses"[4]—as Pizarnik calls her

---

1 Alejandra Pizarnik, "La bucanera de Pernambuco o Hilda la polígrafa," in *Textos de sombra y últimos poemas,* ed. Olga Orozco and Ana Becciú, Buenos Aires, Editorial Sudamericana, 1982, 213–16. See also: Alejandra Pizarnik, "La bucanera de Pernambuco o Hilda la polígrafa," in *Alejandra Pizarnik. Prosa completa,* ed. Ana Becciú, Barcelona, Lumen, 2002, 91–161; Alejandra Pizarnik, "The Lady Buccaneer of Pernambuco or Hilda the Polygraph," trans. Suzanne Jill Levine, *Music & Literature,* no. 6, May 2015, 37–40.
2 "ingenuo (o no)"
3 "piola"
4 "lectotos o lectetas"

"horrendous readers"[1]—that "my unassailability from your shit-
approval will make you read me fullsteam ahead"[2] but also adds,
in the "Prologue of the Forgeress,"[3] that she is looking for a hippopotamus.[4] Clearly a reference to the surrealist imagery and
nonsense to which she was so partial, the figure of the hippopotamus, both massive and unexpected, both awkward and inevitable,
also presages the convulsive and hilarious sense of humor that
characterizes much of Pizarnik's prose output. Far from the lin-
earity that is generally associated with fiction and beyond the field
of influence of the plot, Pizarnikian prose frequently snips the
threads of meaning in language by using fragmented lines or paragraphs. The structure that connects these textual particles responds more to the spatial juxtapositions of a collage than to the
temporal or logical series of events in a story. It thus becomes
clear that Pizarnik's hippopotamus is not merely a humorous or
transgressive subject but also, and perhaps above all, a matter of
form. Material for formal exploration. A method. That this kind
of exploration intensified toward the end of her life, on the level of
both content and form, only adds vital mystery and aesthetic rel-
evance to her vehement desire to write prose. Form, when form
there is, is pure emotion.

Because her desire was indeed vehement. Perhaps this was due
to the fact that, while always a dedicated if iconoclastic reader of
poetry and philosophy, Pizarnik always read prose. She always admired it. By April 1963 she asked, for example, "Can poetry?

1 "horrendos lectores"
2 "mi desasimiento de tu aprobamierda te hará leerme a todo vapor." Translation adapted from: Carolina Depetris, "Crossing Readings on Mysticism:
Alejandra Pizarnik, Antonin Artaud, Miguel de Molinos, Simone Weil and
Georges Bataille," *Revude de littérature comparée* 3, no. 347, 2013, 286.
3 "Proemio de la fraguadora"
4 Pizarnik, *Alejandra Pizarnik. Prosa completa,* 92–97.

Think of Kafka, of Dostoevsky. What poet causes such trembling?"[1]
The poet made equally favorable comments about the great clas-
sics, like Marcel Proust and Virginia Woolf, and other, less fervent
ones about Flaubert and contemporary translations of Françoise
Sagan. What's more, not only was Franz Kafka's diary one of her
bedside books, but her references to his work only increased as
her own diary and life approached their end. Nevertheless, and
notwithstanding her personal proclivities for certain prose writers,
Alejandra Pizarnik repeatedly expressed precise ideas about what
was behind the hippopotamus that introduced the opening pages
of the *Polygraph*. It is about desires in the broadest sense of the
term, as well as specific problems and incomparable reflections on
how to confront, if not resolve, them. It is about the writer reflecting line by line, word by word, on her profession. It is about the
lucid, merciless mind that by 1963 was already contemplating the
relationships between poetry and prose as a problem of fences.
She said: "A problem of the limits in poetry, of fences. Or prose
poetry, definitively. It also needs fences."[2] It is thus about writing
that problematizes a materialization pertaining not only to the
inter but also the intra that coheres but does not establish specific
literary genres. Little by little, with increasing astonishment,
Pizarnik comes to ask herself: "Is it truly necessary, this ritual of
isolated words and lost content to reach the expressive intensity
that this requires?"[3] I believe this is the essential starting point
toward exploring those prosist testimonials that constitute, in the
words of Argentine poet María Negroni, the shadow texts in Ale-

1 "¿La poesía puede? Pensar en Kafka, en Dostoievski. ¿Qué poeta estre-
mece de igual manera?" (Pizarnik, *Diarios*, 333).
2 "Problema de los límites en poesía, de los cercos. . . . O el poema en prosa,
definitivamente. También él necesita cercos" (Pizarnik, *Diarios*, 341).
3 "¿Es preciso el ritual de las palabras aisladas y la pérdida del contenido para
alcanzar la intensidad expresiva que éste requiere?" (Pizarnik, *Diarios*, 448).

jandra Pizarnik's work.[1] For Pizarnik, this is not merely an intellectual exploration, although it was also that; rather, it marked a concrete desire to disrupt the expressive intensity of language as much as possible. Our poet was not given to telling tales for the entertainment of drowsy readers; indeed, she set herself one of the most serious and ultimately most influential writerly challenges in the literary quests of the twentieth century.

The longing for prose is, from the outset, a strange longing. Pizarnik describes her desire in terms of brevity, beauty, and something that escapes the form of the novel. She says: "Moreover, what I would like is to write a really, really short book. Something very beautiful and very short. Not a novel but a chronicle. But I imagine it written in simple, crystalline prose that still allows for all manner of complexities. In short, a kind of prose I'd never know how to write."[2] She repeatedly insists on the writerly construction, on the quality and beauty of the writing as if this were intrinsically negated in prose: "I'm talking about an extremely beautiful prose, a really well-written book. I want my misery to be translated into the utmost possible beauty."[3]

And while poetry has always involved personal misery, prose primarily entails something foreign. Something in a foreign form. Prose, strictly speaking, takes the altered place and establishes the place of the other. Thus, as an exercise in otherness, Pizarnikian

1 María Negroni, *El testigo lúcido. La obra de sombra de Alejandra Pizarnik*, Buenos Aires, Beatriz Viterbo Editora, 2003.

2 "Además lo que yo quisiera es escribir un libro muy, muy breve. Algo muy hermoso y muy breve. No una novela sino una crónica. Pero la imagino en una prosa simple y cristalina, aunque admitiendo todas las complejidades, en fin, aquella prosa que no sabría nunca escribir" (Pizarnik, *Diarios*, 370).

3 "Hablo de una prosa sumamente bella, de un libro muy bien escrito. Quisiera que mi miseria fuera traducida a la mayor belleza posible" (Pizarnik, *Diarios*, 412).

prose makes use of all available tools to court the possibility of "becom[ing] connected to what is outside":[1] the excess of a text without an I. Because when the desire for prose appears, there is also the "painful desire to write about something or someone who isn't me or doesn't have anything to do with me, I want to connect with what is outside, to write and describe, even disfigure (yes, as it will always be)."[2]

This positioning extrinsic to the text, this introduction of referentiality into the body of the text, meant for Pizarnik a thematic foundation, as was true of Elizabeth Báthory, the Hungarian countess with a bloody past. But it was also a formal foundation, as it operated in the appropriation of what she called models or molds. The former becomes quite clear in Pizarnik's many allusions to the unequivocally favorable reception of "La condesa sangrienta" (The Bloody Countess)—a text in which Pizarnik appropriates a text by Valentine Penrose, another poet with surrealist associations who had in turn appropriated texts and documents related to the great bloody dame who murdered, if the historical information serves, approximately 650 peasant girls in her fruitless search for eternal youth.[3] Thus, toward the end of 1968, Alejandra Pizarnik writes: "One of my desires is to write a prose like that of my article about the countess. I believe the need to interrupt the excess of depth—to force myself to meticulously describe the external circumstances of the countess—gave me a freedom (and perhaps a depth) that my own fantasies, unmoored

1 "enlazarse a lo de afuera"
2 "deseo doloroso de escribir sobre algo o alguien que no sea yo ni se relacione conmigo, deseo de enlazarme a lo de afuera, de mirar y describir, aun desfigurando (sí, como siempre será)" (Pizarnik, *Diarios,* 376).
3 Alejandra Pizarnik, "La condesa sangrienta," *Alejandra Pizarnik. Prosa completa,* ed. Ana Becciú, Barcelona, Lumen, 2002, 282–95.

from all concrete detail, never did."[1] Though both Pizarnik and Ana Becciú, editor of her complete works of poetry and prose, included this text in the Articles and Essays section, it still contains a necessarily deceptive wink.

Given the abundance of her "loose and fragmentary fantasies"[2] and an often suffocating self-referentiality, Alejandra Pizarnik transformed the foreign story into a sort of refuge—a structure and an anecdote free of her own self that nevertheless, or perhaps for this very reason, could include her. Copying Beckett in entire sections of *Los poseídos entre lilas* (*The Possessed Among the Lilacs,* translated by Yvette Siegert), or using Penrose's writing on the Hungarian countess, Pizarnik cultivated foreignness in the text, solidarity with the text, by means of commendatory mirrors and ferocious pillagings that paradoxically, as reference molds, fulfilled the stabilizing purpose of prose. The image here is of a hand clinging to the sail that will bear the ship through the storm, or of a hand gripping the window frame so that the subject, looking out, can effectively focus their gaze. Wringing out the mold from the inside, robbing it of itself in full view of the foreign text, but ultimately returning it to itself, Pizarnik made good use of the "betrayals, stalkings, looting, surveillances, and expulsions" that constitute, as Negroni puts it, the world of her writing.[3] Around mid-1966, trying to find a way out of her excess of fragmentary dissemination, Pizarnik rationalized her use of literary molds with her characteristic lucidity and ferocious ambivalence: "Unless I

1 "Uno de mis deseos es escribir en una prosa como la de mi artículo sobre la condesa. Creo que la necesidad de interrumpir el exceso de profundidad—obligarme a detallar circunstancias externas de la condesa—me dio una libertad (y acaso una profundidad) que jamás me concedieron mis propias fantasías, desligadas de todo detalle concreto" (Pizarnik, *Diarios,* 465).

2 "fantasias sueltas y fragmentarias" (Pizarnik, *Diarios,* 416).

3 "traiciones, acechanzas, despojos, vigilancias y expulsiones" (Negroni, *El testigo lúcido,* 80).

put down a foreign story as a model—or mold—and say my piece follows the same number of pages and the same arrangement. Ridiculous."[1]

She did not, however, always need a story. I mean she sought the form of the story, not necessarily its content. When Alejandra Pizarnik wrote "mold,"[2] she was otherwise referring, and with utter precision, to "molde": to the shape of the shoe, once made into a shoe, that wants to walk the world over. Prose, in the Pizarnikian sense, is neither the anecdote nor the content of the story; it is something else, something that, briefly and sublimely, she believes herself to be incapable of writing. It is a prose that casts doubt even on its own ability to communicate. An idea that questions prose's allegedly intrinsic capacity to transmit meaning. Hence, perhaps, her diary entry from May of 1966: "Urgency to start a little book in prose. But its topic could be, precisely, *this vacuous urgency. The need to write and the absence of a need to transmit anything.* It isn't the subject, as I well know, but the fact of having to spend so long revising it once written."[3]

When Alejandra Pizarnik notes her longing for prose, she does so in the position of the writer who is writing in-this-moment. Right here. Right now. What appears in her diary is not the abstracted reflection of her material, but the material itself: How to write it? Why can it not be written? How, if it could be, would it be possible? The incomparable Pizarnik lists the obstacles and

1 "Salvo que ponga un relato ajeno como modelo—o molde—y diga lo mío según la misma cantidad de hojas y la misma distribución. Ridículo" (Pizarnik, *Diarios*, 416).

2 "molde"

3 "Urgencia por comenzar un pequeño libro en prosa. Pero su tema podría ser, precisamente, *esta urgencia vacua. La necesidad de escribir y la no necesidad de transmitir nada.* No se trata del tema, lo sé bien, sino del hecho de tener que estar tanto tiempo, después de haberlo escrito, corrigiéndolo" (Pizarnik, *Diarios*, 414; italics in original).

possibilities, necessarily beginning with the line. The sentence. In an entry in 1968 about the configuration of a sentence, Pizarnik puts forth a view of language that is eminently spatial (perhaps for the same reason Pizarnik tends to make notes to herself about revising a page with the verb "to architect") and also imminently intersubjective. She says:

And what if the unconscious or whatever it is had an exact notion of the configuration of the sentence? Because I bleed out in my efforts to distribute or, better put, to situate terms, as if the sentence were a room full of chairs and my role were to select a chair for each guest. But my torment as hostess lies in the knowledge that everyone knows where they should and want to sit. But if I accept it, what then would be my role in this lugubrious, luxurious party of dying language?[1]

At her party, at the party of language she hosts in the house that does not belong to her, the placement of the chairs, the molds, do exist, but they keep moving around. In order to attend this party she is throwing in her own name, language, in its role as a guest, would have to not know (or pretend not to know) where it is supposed to sit, or even where it wants to sit. The chairs can be there, right in the middle of the room, but both their location and their appointed immobility would be subjected to the subjects of an utterance that, by its very nature, will be a split utterance.

1 "¿Y si el inconsciente o lo que sea, tuviera una exacta noción de la configuración de la frase? Porque yo me desangro en tentativas de distribución o, mejor, de ubicación de los términos, como si la frase fuese un salón lleno de sillas y mi rol consistiera en elegir la silla en que se sentará cada invitado. Pero mi tormento de anfitriona consiste en saber que cada uno sabe dónde debe y quiere sentarse. Pero si lo acepto, ¿cuál sería, entonces, mi rol en esta fiesta lúgubre y lujosa del lenguaje agonizante?" (Pizarnik, *Diarios*, 449).

With these chairs in mind, it becomes entirely understandable that, in order to think in prose, Pizarnik remarks on matters that include the length of her sentences ("I've observed, re-reading my unsent letters to C. C., that my long sentences are disastrous"),[1] as well as the system she has not invented to contain them ("My study of prose poetry is modified by not knowing whether I should use a folder or loose pages to conduct it"),[2] and her preoccupation with the space between lines ("Prose poetry: the need for double spaces. At least for my 'style'").[3] The question of the line between poetry and prose acquires here a material presence that is both problematic and sensual. It is not, of course, a matter of monitoring the limits of one or the other, or even of waving a vehement finger in their direction, but of identifying the mechanisms that may accommodate for its inverted possibility. This is where her prose poems are resolved in plural and consequently proliferate. Pizarnik elaborates on various occasions, for example, about:

Prose poems that are open (with silences) and closed, compact, almost without periods and new paragraphs.

Prose poems that are very brief, brief like aphorisms (Rimbaud: "Phrases"). . . .

In prose poems, spaces are necessary (each paragraph a phrase like Rimbaud's. Or various phrases. But all within three or four lines. And double-spaced. Otherwise you have to forget

1 "He observado, releyendo las cartas a C. C. que no le he enviado, que mis oraciones extensas son desastrosas" (Pizarnik, *Diarios*, 370).
2 "Mi estudio sobre el poema en prosa se altera por no saber usar una carpeta u hojas sueltas para realizarlo" (Pizarnik, *Diarios*, 420).
3 "Poemas en prosa: necesidad de los espacios dobles. Al menos para mi «estilo»" (Pizarnik, *Diarios*, 419).

about the economy of language and write in the most fluid way that exists: Miller).[1]

In pursuit of this prose that is an altered refuge or an antidote to its fragmentary dissemination, Pizarnik alludes to and ridicules— the ambivalence is always there—other qualities of so-called normal prose. "This prose of my diary," she notes, "is much like what's called normal prose. Why, when I write, don't I try to appeal to it? I think my correspondence with C. C. was good for me because it forced me to write to him with clarity. Is clarity a virtue? I know no virtues. I only know desires."[2] In addition, she continues to weigh the problem of the unit that is, clearly, a problem of structure: "The trouble is this: where can I find, in my loose compositions, an axis or something like a spine? Until now, it has been the method of loose compositions. Now I would like something more extensive, like *The Countess*."[3]

All it takes is a glance at some of the lewd, daring pages of *Hilda la polígrafa* to realize that when Alejandra Pizarnik talks about prose, she is really talking, as with her own poetry, about some-

1 Poemas en prosa abiertos (con silencios) y cerrados, compactos y casi sin puntos y apartes. Poemas en prosa muy breves, breves como aforismos (Rimbaud: "Phrases"). . . . En el poema en prosa los espacios son necesarios (cada párrafo una frase como las de Rimbaud. O varias frases. Pero todo dentro de tres o cuatro líneas. Y con espacios dobles. En caso contrario hay que olvidarse de la economía del lenguaje y escribir del modo más fluido que existe: Miller)" (Pizarnik, *Diarios,* 418).

2 "Esta prosa de mi diario se parece a lo que llaman una prosa normal. ¿Por qué, cuando escribo, no trato de apelar a ella? Pienso que mi correspondencia con C. C. me hacía bien pues me obligaba a escribirle con claridad. ¿Es una virtud la claridad? Ignoro cuáles son las virtudes. Sólo conozco los deseos" (Pizarnik, *Diarios,* 465).

3 "El problema es el siguiente: ¿cómo descubrir, en mis composiciones sueltas, un eje o algo a modo de columna vertebral? Hasta ahora fue el método de las composiciones sueltas. Ahora quisiera algo mucho más extenso, como *La condesa*" (Pizarnik, *Diarios,* 451).

thing else. As if the longing for prose, which she knows is impossible, were more like a longing for its own impossibility. Or as if the longing she knows to be impossible were becoming ever more impossible, thus prompting more longing, when confronted with the comically anti-communicative invective of proses with questionable axes and rhizomatic points. As if she liked to fail. As if that failure constituted, after all, the victorious wink of her longing. This one.

# 53

## *The Refuge Is a Work in the Shape of a Dwelling*

### (SECOND CHAPTER)

Toward the very end of her life, a couple years before receiving the Guggenheim Fellowship and, almost simultaneously, the Rockefeller Fellowship, Alejandra Pizarnik wrote in her diary what reads like an overdue feigned apology or a simple account of the facts or a sort of anticipatory resignation: "I didn't want to be these fragments. But since I must, since I cannot, do not want to be someone else, I must re-write or type up one fragment a day."[1]

From afar, from the position of someone who knows what happened on September 25, 1972, these sentences could not be more ominous. The sentences also state the obvious: that Alejandra Pizarnik's fragmentation always was, more than a random and/or rational choice, a condemnation. Not a style: a fate. That the form of Pizarnik's writing is also, and perhaps above all, its crux. And that crux is, why not?, the one she always wanted to reach. And yet, from this far-off apparition that crosses barriers of time and space,

1 "Yo no quise ser estos fragmentos. Pero, puesto que debo, puesto que no puedo, no quiero ser otra, debo o tengo que reescribir o copiar a máquina un fragmento por día" (Pizarnik, *Diarios,* 453).

I can see her bent over her desk, copying out in her tiny letters—
the handwriting that some described as a line of ants—a daily fragment. With the discipline or obsession warranted by the case at
hand, I write these words in order to watch her first select and
then copy that fragment—the one that says what she would say
differently. Always differently.

It is true, or at least asserted by many of her diary entries, that
Pizarnik did not want to be "those fragments."[1] It is true that she
described them as "paltry leftovers"[2] that exhibited her physical
and mental limitations as well as her lack of discipline, her disor-
derliness, and the self-absorption that frequently terrorized her.
"My mind is weak," she stated in an entry on June 3, 1963, "hence
my reading 'method' and the brevity of my poems. There is a total
scattering: only fragments that 'come out of nowhere.'"[3] Likewise,
critical and hurt, she lashed out at "the indiscipline and disorder
[that] lead to an awareness of the void"—although she claimed
she could work up to ten hours a day, as when she was writing *La
condesa sangrienta*.[4] Also subject to her displeasure was that "fear
of my monstrous thinking about myself, of my self-complacency
and, at the same time, of my extreme hardness. I want to be serene. I am trembling as I write this."[5] In opposition to such states
of extreme unease and profound self-doubt as a writer, confronted
with the trembling that accompanied her desire for serenity,

1 "esos fragmentos"
2 "sobras miserables"
3 "Mi mente es débil, de allí mi «método» de lectura y la brevedad de mis
poemas. Hay una dispersión total: sólo fragmentos que «vienen desde la
nada»" (Pizarnik, *Diarios*, 339–40).
4 "la indisciplina y el desorden [que] conducen a la toma de conciencia del
vacío" (Pizarnik, *Diarios*, 340).
5 "miedo de mi monstruoso pensar en mí, de mi complacencia para conmigo
y, a la vez, de mi extrema dureza. Quiero estar serena. Esto lo escribo tem-
blando" (Pizarnik, *Diarios*, 363).

Pizarnik imagined prose. That is why she invented it. That is why she longed for it. "Constrict yourself," she said, "demand of yourself a little mental continuity."[1] Is this where her desire, or her fear, began?

Again and again, however, her journey toward prose would be questioned or deflected or impeded by her own way of writing, her way of living, and even her way of speaking. On more than one occasion, for example, Pizarnik blamed everything on her knowledge, comprehensive or otherwise, of the basic rules of language: "Everything comes down to the fact that I don't know grammar."[2] Sometimes, too, she alludes to the same problem as always: "How dare I write in a language I do not know?"[3] In still other moments, moments of greater contemplation and analysis, Pizarnik formulated long lists of reasons, both intellectual and vital, why prose escaped her. In 1964, the year she returned to Argentina after four difficult but productive years in Paris, she reflected:

> My lack of rhythm when I write. Disjointed phrases. Impossibility of forming sentences, of conserving the traditional grammatical structure. I'm missing the *subject*. Then I'm missing the verb. What's left is a mutilated predicate, tattered attributes I don't know who or what to give them to. This is due to a lack of meaning in my internal elements. No. It's more like a problem of attention. And, above all, a sort of castration of the ear: I cannot perceive the melody of a sentence. That's also where my curious intonation, my oral difficulties come from. What I'm

1 "Constreñirse, exigirse un poco de continuidad mental" (Pizarnik, *Diarios*, 340).
2 "Todo se debe a que no sé gramática" (Pizarnik, *Diarios*, 384).
3 "¿cómo podría yo atreverme a escribir en una lengua que no conozco?" (Pizarnik, *Diarios*, 456).

saying here has come to be my emblem. My oral difficulties are caused by my distance from reality.[1]

Two things stand out:

1) The internal elements: the subject (which is what is missing), the verb (of lack), the predicate (castrated here like the ear). And the problem of attention.
2) The distance from reality: "Primary problems: organization and time."[2] "Mental disorder from having conversed for two hours with my mother on the most important topic: order."[3] And money, the oft-mentioned financial problem. Because after she returned from Europe, though before she received prestigious international fellowships, Pizarnik had to live with her mother and be supported by her— two things that, over time, became a source of anxiety. The curse of being a poet.

In the face of these major obstacles, both internal and external, in the face of these trifles of circumstance and action,

1 "Mi falta de ritmo cuando escribo. Frases desarticuladas. Imposibilidad de formar oraciones, de conservar la tradicional estructura gramatical. Es que me falta el *sujeto*. Luego, me falta el verbo. Queda un predicado mutilado, quedan harapos de atributos que no sé a quién o a qué regalar. Esto se debe a la falta de sentido de mis elementos internos. No. Más bien se trata de una dificultad de la atención. Y, sobre todo, de una suerte de castración del oído: no puedo percibir la melodía de una frase. De ahí, también, mi curiosa entonación, mis dificultades orales. Esto que digo viene a ser mi emblema. Mis dificultades orales provienen de mi lejanía de la realidad" (Pizarnik, *Diarios*, 364).
2 "Problemas principales: organización y tiempo" (Pizarnik, *Diarios*, 450).
3 "Desorden mental por haber conversado dos horas con mi madre acerca del tema más importante: el orden" (Pizarnik, *Diarios*, 439).

then, was the prose—the prose that Pizarnik saw, without res-
ervation and perhaps even without any metaphors, as a house.
She wrote in 1969, with respect to the construction of prose as
a dwelling: "If you're going to write stories and novels, you must
plan, make blueprints (a few or many, it doesn't matter). You
have to plan, order into chapters, know in advance what will be
said. At the typewriter's whim, prose emerges as a sample of er-
rant language. But a book, like a house, entails a true plan, as
well as industriousness and patience."[1] Here, we must note that
Pizarnik is not employing her well-known sense of irony; rather,
as in other cases and always in relation to prose, she is explicitly associating a means of writing—a mold, to use her term—
with the security and protection of a home. "When it comes to
prose, I am thrown into confusion," she admits. "But I could
start with very short stories. No, I want a refuge. The refuge is a
work in the shape of a dwelling. Is this diary—let us call it—not
one?"[2]

Accustomed as I am to narrators who long, with a truly vehement longing, to access poetry, it does not cease to astonish me
that a poet, a great poet like Alejandra Pizarnik, describes prose
as a house she does not have. It surprises me, I mean, that by
making prose into a safe house, she refers to poetry, by sheer con-

1 "Para hacer cuentos y novelas es preciso *planear,* hacer proyectos (pocos o
muchos, no importa). Hay que planificar, ordenar en capítulos, saber de an-
temano qué se va a decir. Al azar de la máquina de escribir surgen prosas que
son una muestra de lenguaje errante. Pero un libro, como una casa, implica
una verdadera planificación y además laboriosidad y paciencia" (Pizarnik,
*Diarios,* 480).
2 "Cuando se trata de prosa entro en confusión. Pero podría empezar con
cuentos muy breves. No, yo quiero un refugio. El refugio es una obra en
forma de morada. ¿Acaso no lo es este—digamos—diario?" (Pizarnik, *Diarios,* 368).

trast, as exposure to the elements. A kind of danger. A defense-lessness. And this becomes even more surprising if you consider that, at least in *La bucanera de Pernambuco* though also in *Los poseídos entre lilas,* Pizarnikian prose abounds with "collections of paraphrases, impossible translations, collages of idioms. . . . Like a circus in which the bearded woman, the clown, the contortionist, the *écuyère* with her white tutu cohabitate; combinations of diverse and also nonexistent languages are surrendered here in a linguistic game whose post-Babelic or apocalyptic calling points, once again, to the Latin American Neo-baroque."[1] From the outside—that is from the position of a reader of Alejandra Pizarnik's poetry and prose—it would be truly difficult to grant the latter the stability and protection of a refuge. In fact, María Negroni, an attentive reader of Pizarnik, suggests a contrary relationship: before "the delight of the profanatory gesture in the prose texts," Pizarnik's poetry "is written on the basis of a 'cleansing' operation."[2] As if, confronted with the celebratory and irreverent courage of her texts in prose, the poetic miniatures, already cleansed of leftovers and excess, constituted the true refuge. The intangible house.

Should we believe the poet? I wonder. Which one? I respond. In any case, I know, with the author's generally limited knowledge of her own text, that Alejandra Pizarnik never tired of inscribing in her diary, of embodying in her diary, this longing—never satisfied,

1 "las colecciones de paráfrasis, las traducciones imposibles, los collages de idiotismos. . . . Como en un circo en el cual conviven la mujer barbuda, el *clown,* la contorsionista, la *écuyère* con su tutú blanco, se dan aquí combinaciones de idiomas diversos y también inexistentes, en un juego lingüístico cuya vocación postbabélica o apocalíptica apunta, una vez más, al neobarroco latinoamericano" (Negroni, *El testigo lúcido,* 110–11).
2 "la alegría del gesto profanatorio de los textos en prosa se escribe sobre la base de un operativo de 'limpieza'" (Negroni, *El testigo lúcido,* 113).

in her view—for prose. In 1968, still in Paris, she wrote: "But among other troubles, I suffer from the very vivisection of isolated words. As if those gems with which I contemplate my texts had as their end goal to release me from the precariousness of the prose I write with."[1]

---

1 "Pero entre otros problemas, padezco el de la revivisección de las palabras aisladas. Como si esas joyas con que contemplo mis escritos tuvieran por finalidad excusarme de la precariedad de la prosa que escribo" (Pizarnik, *Diarios*, 456).

# 54

## *It's as If I Had Discovered the Intolerable and Impossible Thing About Poetry*

### (SOMETHING LIKE A CONCLUSION)

She longed for the little, well-written book; the staggeringly beautiful book whose subject was language itself. An intense book that would keep her, for hours, full days, years if possible, constructing her own place. A book in prose that was not a novel but a house. She longed for what she always produced. In Spanish, she said, there was no one who would serve as a model. Not Paz or Cortázar or Borges. Perhaps only Rulfo, but Rulfo, she also said, was "extremely musical."[1] There was nothing in Latin America like Nerval's *Aurélia,* but above all she wanted a book that was not Argentine. She longed. A book that was eminently hers: the beginning of the P of Pizarnik. A minuscule book. A book for the little girls who sit in the palm of her hand to swear or pray.

Judging by her comments on the topic that appear in her diary,

---

1 "sumamente musical" (Pizarnik, *Diarios,* 412).

this longing, made explicit since 1954 (included in a to-do list covering the subsequent forty days), remained a thwarted longing till the very end. Her longing for prose, that is, was always, and until the very end, a longing. Nevertheless, the torrent of words she wrote on the relationships between poetry and prose, on the material and experiential mechanisms involved once one decides, or needs, to connect these two kinds of writing, are among the most overtly prophetic and sharply provocative of her essayistic output. Pizarnik writes in the "normal prose"[1] of her diary about the challenges and scopes that prefigure the prose of her prose; there she problematizes and executes it, describes it and judges it, deplores it ("Or, perhaps, I want to give my strange texts a special visa. As they are incomprehensible, at least let the verbal magic save them").[2] She wants it. She courts it. She Pizarniks it.

In this sense, it is noteworthy that Pizarnik's concern is not, strictly speaking, prose, but the agitated and combinable site of prose poetry—a form she described as having imposed itself on her; a form not chosen, or chosen, in any case, after the fact. From the beginning, when she separates herself from the novelistic enterprise by deeming it contrary to her nature, Pizarnik's longing is an adjacent longing, illegitimate and vertiginous; for the same reason, it opens its doors to insolence, play, humor, and, above all, to the probabilities of sex. It is a longing embedded both in the poetry of Perlongher and Thénon and in texts by Lautremont and Artaud. It is a crazy, strange, unclassifiable longing. Most of all, it is an altered longing for otherness: to

1 "prosa normal"
2 "O, tal vez, quiero dar un visado especial a mis textos raros. Puesto que son incomprensibles, que los salve, aunque sea, la magia verbal" (Pizarnik, *Diarios*, 456).

fix the external subject/object in order to introduce it, with all its movement, with all its eventuality, into the interiority of her own text. It is a primary sexual longing. It is the longing sparked by stumbling upon that "intolerable and impossible" limit of poetry.[1]

1 "intolerable e imposible" (Pizarnik, *Diarios*, 459).

# 55

---

## Coda

### (THE OBLIGATORY QUESTION)

"Who's speaking? Who the hell is speaking?"[1]

—ALEJANDRA PIZARNIK,
"La justa de los pompones" (The Pompom Joust)

---

1 «¿Quién habla? ¿Quién carajos habla?» (Pizarnik, *Alejandra Pizarnik. Prosa completa*, 148).

# V

## Valerio's True Reports

It emanates from future violence into the past, into the present of those of us who are waiting in our own past, like a sinister outpouring that our senses can detect without a single sniff. Violence is a thing of human bodies; of bodies awaiting the unawaitable: what already happened, what happened abruptly, what will never happen at all.

—SALVADOR ELIZONDO

# 56

## Death's Business Is to Strip

Crime strips. The wound betrays the victim: there, amid its folds and shadows, we can glimpse the other life of their life, the secret, subterranean life, the shameful passion, the calculation error, the inconceivable habit, the particular lack. The weapon exposes the perpetrator: the blade, the cost, the stratagem behind the occasion, the furor, the viciousness. But the crime also reveals the onlooker: the one who passes by and freezes with fear; the one who closes their eyes, scandalized; the one who walks on, hoping to protect their indifference or their hurry; the one who succumbs to wide-eyed fascination. Valerio hadn't chosen to see the castrated men, but as soon as his gaze first rested there, on the devastation of what he was missing, on the indescribable violence of what he was missing, he knew this homicide could easily be the negative of some photograph of his life. In the future, perhaps. In the past. There was something about castration that forced him to consider personal danger, the threat against his own body. A primordial scene. A foundational fear.

My name isn't Valerio. He said this in silence, inside his head, as he delved deeper and deeper into the scene of the crime. He was attracted, as he had rarely been before, by the setting: the red of the blood, the glow of the streetlights, the low hum of murmuring voices. By then, he'd seen all kinds of murders, but none so stylized or so explicitly sexual. The body, more than sprawled in an alley that reeked of urine, gave the impression of being staged. A legendary drama. The blood, red and heavy, looked artificial. And the genitals, absent, severed with surgical precision, commanded attention. By not being there, they were more there than life, more there than death. It wasn't until later, when, for reasons related to this case and in collaboration with the Detective, he began to study the poetry of Alejandra Pizarnik, that he reconsidered what he'd seen: death's business—Alejandra was right—was to strip.

Years later, he'd remember those days as the most difficult days of his life. He'd describe them as such, expressly: *they were the most difficult days of my life.* He'd recall them at the slightest provocation, especially when fear, any fear, accosted him with its two-toned spikes or long tail. Alone or accompanied, Valerio would then retreat into his inner place, where he kept an altar to his most trifling terrors, and fall silent. Motionless. Absent. Statue of artifice. Earthly monument. The silence, that silence, would be interrupted only by a question: how is it that I came to think my name wasn't Valerio? Recalling this absurd, incomprehensible, entirely useless rejection would trigger the raucous laughter with which he'd return to where he really was: his present. His name: Valerio. To Say: Valerio.

# 57

## *Can a Poem Take the Place of a Dog's Piss?*

He went to the Detective he was working with and told her, in his characteristically measured tone, what he'd seen and what he knew. After an initial review of the facts: the man found lying there, in the space they would soon begin to call the Alley of the Castrated Men, was not exactly naked. He was still wearing a pair of patent leather shoes and a shirt that had been white until it was stained with the red of his death. A black briefcase had been found nearby, its contents intact. A wristwatch. A class ring. Except for the pants that had been yanked down to his knees, everything else looked normal. The man was, as he'd soon learn, a journalist of little renown; a bachelor who was just making his first forays with a local paper, often writing for the sports section. He was, and he confirmed this himself out of sheer curiosity, more or less his age. There had been no rape. None of what he gradually discovered, first at the scene of the crime and then in his breakneck but methodical investigations, surprised him. A man had a penis and then he no longer had one. A man bled to death, alone, in the shelter of night, in an alley. A man without a penis, a castrated man, was found by a woman. The woman, that woman, summoned all the others, stripping them. Who are you? I'm not Valerio.

And the Detective, of course, had cackled at his last remark.

Months before, when he hadn't even imagined being part of the team responsible for the case of the Castrated Men, when he'd only just decided to take a job he hadn't sought, or which he'd only half sought, more dejected than interested, as an assistant to a detective in the Department of Homicide Investigation, that laughter had startled him. It was a hoarse, lewd sound that seemed to come from very far away, traveling sluggishly along dirt roads under the ceaseless lashes of a summer storm. The sound, which verged on an explosive cackle, had stopped, for reasons he would never be able to clarify, just before. The slammed door. The book shut, never to be opened again. The end of trust. Such a sudden shift from pleasure to enclosure had forced him to reevaluate the woman before him. She had a secret. She was living with a secret. He sensed this, and then, almost immediately, he believed it. A kind of faith. He pictured her body under her blue uniform, admired her unmanicured but expressive hands, inhaled the fragrance of her hair, and gave thanks, though he never knew to whom, for the schedule he'd been offered in the form of employment. That initial laughter, clipped and hard, incredulous, pensive, became the melody of his days—the easy ones, and then the ones he didn't yet know would be the most difficult of his life.

The Detective—this is what he thought after a couple weeks working alongside her—liked to lose. He soon learned that she'd been working there for years, in the basement that never saw any natural light, without giving it a moment's thought. Without complaining much. No promotions. No raises. The basement turned sarcophagus. They were assigned two kinds of cases: everyday cases (petty drug dealing, for instance) and cases so outlandish or incomprehensible (the disappearance of a woman from China in a whirlwind, among others) that higher-ranking investigators had discreetly rejected. The Detective hadn't distinguished herself by solving cases quickly or otherwise, but she did write long reports full of questions and details that pleased the aesthetic sensibilities of the chief of the Department of Homicide Investigation. They sometimes spoke of authors who always managed to solve cases within the rectangle of the page, or, more often, of television shows where men and women who didn't resemble them in any way solved, with a profound sense of duty and enviable physical fitness, flashy cases of international importance. The Detective would then laugh the laughter that Valerio associated with her. And then, in her office, she'd start shuffling through papers and scribbling possible trails to follow or, in turn, their impossible conclusions.

The runner who would become their first witness, the key witness in the case of the Castrated Men, would repeat over and over in her initial testimony that she didn't want to see anything like that ever again. Ever. Never again. Watching her, listening to her with absolute attention, Valerio would consider for the first time and with great terror, a terror he hadn't experienced until then, that they may have been dealing with the deranged work of a serial killer. Later, when he confirmed that she was talking to herself, when he had no doubt that the woman was in constant communication with beings who were themselves impossible, he'd question it once more.

The first city newspaper headline to take on the matter in the evening edition said: GRUESOME SCENE! MAN CASTRATED IN ALLEY.

Hours after he'd visited the scene of the crime, Valerio would realize he was familiar with that kind of terror after all. It was something shapeless but recognizable that moved through him like food, with the tang of stomach-bound saliva. Once there, it spread around the middle of the body and stopped moving. A stagnation. A being and not being. Something he had once called "the wingbeat." He'd felt it most particularly, he knew, in situations of abandonment. In his moments of greatest self-doubt. When everything felt stuck. It was something he remembered from adolescence, from just before adolescence. The unpeeling.

"You're white as a sheet, Valerio," the Detective had said, catching him staring at the opposite wall, papers motionless in his hands.

Valerio turned to look at her as if the desert sun were suddenly falling vertically into the basement where they worked. He sat up. He passed along the latest information: a copy of the Pizarnik poem they'd discovered, painted in nail polish, on a brick in the alley.

"It's pretty sick, that's for sure." The Detective's words gave him a pang. He agreed. And he saw a long procession of unanswered questions file along before him.

"What if it were someone just like you or me?" he asked for the sake of asking.

"That wouldn't be so bad," the woman said ironically, and she laughed that laughter of dirt roads and storms. It was then, just when he saw that her laugh wouldn't explode into a cackle, that she reminded him of his sister. "It's always someone like you or me, Valerio. You should know that by now."

The terror, the kind he was in fact familiar with, returned intact. He saw his sister's face close to his own, and then, again, he sensed the loneliness of the moment when the face became the neck and the neck, in the distance now, transformed into something smaller and smaller. The head of a pin. Hundreds of angels dancing in the center of it. And then, there, in the center of that dense, movable center, of that center that was also about to disappear, the Detective's face emerged.

"We're dealing with something truly difficult here," she murmured to both of them. "Whoever did this chose the place long before, don't you think? Do we have any information? I'm sure they chose it and marked it with this"—she lifted the copy of the poem—"'like a dog. Can a poem take the place of a dog's piss?' In any case, he focused on waiting for that man who—you can tell from his face—comes from far away, looking for something without yet knowing what it is. Who does that?"

"Someone very patient," Valerio reflected aloud. "Someone who believes in poetry. Someone who trusts the blade of every word. Someone with manual dexterity. In short, someone twisted, like everyone else, but with a certain kind of mental map. Books. Specific tastes. Someone who walks a lot, who walks nearby."

"Is it a woman or a man, Valerio?" the Detective asked unexpectedly, not taking her eyes off him.

"If you put it like that, I'd have to say that it's a woman and a man simultaneously." He fell silent, waiting for an answer that didn't come. "But who truly isn't a woman and a man at the same time?"

"Who found the body? What's that professor's name again?"

Valerio watched her pick up her jacket and stride toward the basement exit. That, he thought, exactly like that, was how he'd seen his sister for the last time. The swiftness, then a futile star.

------------

# 58

## The Incredible Shrinking Woman

By the time he was thinking of those days as the most difficult of his life, Valerio would also recall that moment: the moment when his sister's face and the Detective's face became one. He'd walk in the shade of the poplar trees, past benches full of people, along the edges of lugubrious parks. He'd keep walking down city streets, which would continue to be his favorite method to ensure that the interruptions of daily life would allow him access to unexpected forms of reasoning, and he'd wonder whether the difficulty of those days, which he'd still find unbearable then, still painful, might have something to do with that exchange of faces.

"The things you'll do," the old man would mutter, "to refuse abandonment. To turn it into something else."

And he'd stay there, motionless in the final glow before the sun set, imagining the hundreds of angels on the head of his pin.

The second murder caught them off guard but didn't surprise them. This time, the Pizarnik poem had appeared in the second victim's closed fist, indicating, according to the Detective, that the murderer, man or woman, was prepared to take other risks. The planning was explicit in the careful clipping of each letter used to copy out the poem: "NOW THEN: Who will stop plunging their hands in search of tributes for the forgotten girl. The cold will pay. The wind will pay. As will the rain. And the thunder. *For Aurora and Julio Cortázar.*" The urge to continue seeped with utter clarity into the threat of these words. In this case, form and content made the same declaration: the murders wouldn't stop.

The second victim's neighbor would testify that he'd heard something, something loud enough to be heard but strange enough to not be understood. There were moans; he was sure of that. Moans, in the opinion of a neighbor poking around at night, that were sexual in nature.

"A normal thing," he would add, as if rushing to conceal what was already in plain sight, "for a young, single man. Having nighttime guests, I mean."

The Detective and Valerio would exchange glances at that moment.

"Guests?" she would ask him in a knowing tone.

"Guests, yes," the neighbor would murmur. "Male and female. You know how things are these days."

When he saw the first corpse, Valerio feared there would be others, but he never imagined that, days later, he'd be walking beside the Detective to discuss the matter of the dedications. They'd never walked together before. They knew they both walked when they needed to think, if not better then at least differently, but ever since they started working as a team, they'd kept their outings separate. The Castrated Men changed that, too: their solitary wanderings. Bundled up against the wind that roared in with dust on its back, they set out, and they soon fell into a swift pace.

"I'm concerned about how clean the crime scene is," she remarked by way of introduction. "This sort of thing, a dismemberment of this kind, should produce more blood. Blood spilled everywhere. But you saw it yourself: just a puddle. A large puddle, yes, but just a puddle under the body."

"Unless there was no struggle," Valerio ventured, only to contradict himself. "Which would be strange in a case like this. We'll have to carefully test for sedatives. Various drugs."

"Or it could be the work of an expert," the Detective interrupted. "A surgeon. A highly skilled butcher. A chef."

"Flesh. Food. A tasting. That's what it all sounds like, doesn't it?"

"A banquet we weren't invited to."

"Or that we have been invited to, Valerio, but no one told us the menu or the address," she replied, pensive. "I'm also concerned about the dedication." She showed it to him again. "Or is this what all scholarly murderers are like? Look—it's not just the text copied out, but the dedication, too. *Aurora and Julio Cortázar.* Why both? To emphasize there was nothing sexual between them, the female author of the dedication and the male half of the acknowledged pair? Was that Julio married to that Aurora? Are there texts of hers, too?"

"He was a librarian," Valerio cut in, knowing as he did that her questions could go on forever. "A librarian scrupulously murdered, if I may, in the same house where he often received nighttime guests, both male and female."

"Male and female guests possibly interested in faithfulness to the textual citation," she added with her typical irony, and unwittingly began, at the same time, to scrape a coin against the wall they walked along. Valerio found himself distracted by the childlike, entirely automatic gesture.

"Male and female guests, let's say," she continued, "as well-read as the murderer, male or female, who doesn't forget to mention who the poem they've copied is dedicated to."

The lines left by the coin on the half-painted concrete wall seemed to register the rise and fall of the conversation. An inner rhythm. Something commeasurable.

"Male and female guests," she insisted, "who could have been suitable for an experiment." She turned to look at him as if she were already somewhere else. "Like in a sect. Right? Extreme swingers. There are two or three clubs like that in the city, aren't there?"

"They could fine you for that," Valerio said in a scornful voice when he finally dared call attention to what she was doing.

Her only answer was to furrow her brow and slip the coin back into her coat pocket. Then, as if this had been their arrangement from the very beginning, she said goodbye and set off on her own without another word. Valerio paused to watch her. He thought the Detective was a woman with the hang-ups of a little girl. He imagined her, though he didn't know why, as an incredible shrinking woman: someone or something he could keep, like she kept her coin, inside his jacket pocket.

Days later, always at home and always alone, he would start taking notes on the Incredible Shrinking Woman. He'd assign her a height: eleven centimeters. He'd arrange the setting for her first appearance: on the tabletop, behind the saltshaker, on a day when he was eating lentil soup. Without warning. Without origins. A simple surge. Bristol, 1699. Captain William Prescott. He'd clothe her in dolls' dresses he'd search for, with some desperation, with some morbid urgency, in the suitcases his sister had left in the family closet. He'd secure a group of friends for her: the she-bird who sang in a neighbor's cage, the long-tongued blue lizard, children's fingers. He'd give her a name: the Incredible Shrinking Woman. The sight of her would bring him immense pleasure, a nearly unimaginable pleasure. He'd listen intently to her soft voice, the voice of an adult woman. Like Lemuel Gulliver in Lilliput, he'd quickly develop a combination of tenderness and sympathy for the fragility he associated with her size. He'd place her in the palm of his hand, lift her up to his eyes, and watch her leap into the void. He'd take a long time to organize a story for her. To tell it to her.

# 59

## I'm Your Equal

He struggled to look at the third murder. They'd run around frantically, asking questions, reading messages from a crazy woman, following possible clues, hypothesizing connections, and so, when the phone rang with the call they knew was coming at some point in the future, they kept distressingly silent. Time was running out. Time was running faster than they were. The murderer or murderess. Death itself was far swifter.

Observing the third body in the street, a body so close to another line of Pizarnik's, this one written in lipstick across the pavement, Valerio had to eliminate from his suspect list the weepy woman who'd sworn she was the wife of the librarian they knew received nighttime guests, male and female, in his bachelor pad. He'd deemed jealousy a motive as he compared her case, still hypothetical, with other cases that had taken place both in their country and abroad: in most of them, jealous women had grabbed a kitchen knife and sliced off, with unimaginable rage, the penis from the unfaithful body. As soon as they started to investigate the third man, he was forced to accept there was no connection between them at all, which meant the jealous woman hypothesis, effective in one case, proved entirely useless, even scandalous and sexist, in explaining the series of murders that could now officially be referred to as serial.

"We're in the presence of an aesthete," the Detective murmured. "An obsessive aesthete who wants to send us a message about the body, the male body, and the letters of the alphabet."

She said all this as if in a trance while Valerio discarded his own hypothesis, and the investigative team cordoned off the area around the third castrated man. She said all this crouched down, pressing the tip of her index finger to the lipsticked letters, distributed carefully enough to cover much of the pavement.

"We're in the presence of an aesthete who wants to send us a message about the male body and the letters of the alphabet but with women's objects." Her voice had the timbre of a retraction.

Valerio thought of the nail polish, the cut-out letters, the lipstick.

"A man posing as a woman? A woman posing as a woman?"

The Detective patted him on the back for the very first time.

He would be responsible for identifying the similarities: three young men with pleasing phenotypes but otherwise ordinary. Three middle-class professionals more or less affiliated with the humanities. Three single men with exquisite taste and a certain interest, or the possibility of a certain interest, in matters of art and poetry, especially contemporary. Three grown sons. Three independent beings with a room of their own and expensive shoes. Three bodies that had known pleasure and abandon and heat and wind. Three stories of which little was known and much imagined. And each one, whether outside his home like man number one and man number three, or inside his home like man number two, had had a run-in with the murderer or murderess. They'd stirred his or her interest or cruelty or desire. From the beginning, without really reaching an agreement on this point, they would assume that the murderer or murderess and the three victims had previously known each other. Since there was no indication they'd been dragged or taken by force, they'd assume the victims had voluntarily followed the murderer or murderess to those dark or distant places where a poem by Alejandra Pizarnik, as they surely finally realized, awaited them. And as the crime scenes were extraordinarily organized, minimalist even, they would assume that between the murderer or murderess and the victim had been forged, perhaps by dint of seduction, a bond of apparent trust. They would assume that none of what the castrated men had known or imagined about the world up until that fateful day had prepared them to suspect what was coming: the slash that would take their masculinity to another place, somewhere they'd never been before. The cut. The scissura. The scrupulous ferocity.

"Who knows three men like that at the same time?" he wondered aloud while going over his notes. "Everyone," he answered at once, defeated. "I know three men like that. Or more."

Days later, when the messages that someone signed with a woman's name—with the names of several women, really—began to arrive, they'd all get used to speaking of the killer in the feminine. No one, however, would find a suitable grammatical way to masculinize *the victim,* which was surely why—although it was surely for many other reasons, too—the newspapers would call it the case of the Castrated Men. A distant musical resonance. Tragic qualities. The evening papers, however, would single out the particular inefficiency of the Detective in this case, and Valerio would remember this stage of the investigation as the time when he became the bodyguard of and spy on a professor who often held long conversations with beings he couldn't see, and also with the Woman Who Resembled His Sister. A professor who ran. Someone ready to flee.

In those days of cautious persecution and incredible weariness, full of tension, full of terror, he would gradually expand his knowledge of the Incredible Shrinking Woman. She liked salt, for instance, liked licking its broad surface and kicking at its rocky heft. She preferred sleeping in the she-bird's nest. She favored the lewd games of the lizard, who used its long tongue to tickle various parts of her body. She could stay underwater for a long time. Indeed, she'd spend entire evenings in the fish tank, contorting her body beside the orange fish that would wrap her in its long, ductile fins. He'd watch her through the misted glass; he'd gesture to her. Arms outstretched. Palms flat. Come, he seemed to say to her. Valerio imagined she wanted to tell him something, that the Incredible Shrinking Woman had a message for him. But the days passed, those days, the days he would later remember as an impasse in the case of the Castrated Men; the days that, in the near future, he'd fervently scold the Detective, without receiving any message in return.

She had a secret. The Detective had a secret. Her cackle betrayed her. Her absolute concentration on cases that were difficult to solve, sustaining a hope that would consistently falter in everyone else, betrayed her. Inevitably. More than anything else, what betrayed her was her accent: that extra thump at the end of words that emerged in dreams. Every crime she investigated betrayed her. The hands she didn't groom, the meanderings she now undertook, once again, alone. The composition of her reports. The way she obsessively—if possible—ordered him to protect someone else. A woman. Her reflections. The body he pictured under the blue uniform. The grace he'd attribute to a silence that others would dismiss as sullen. The unthinkability of her approach, swift as a slash, and then the sudden remoteness that left him with nothing. An amputation. A lethal theft. Years later, reflecting on all this, on all this he'd then describe as his past, he'd think he'd followed the Detective back to her house, that he'd undressed her and kissed her and penetrated her and embraced her because he was sure she had a secret. Because she wanted to share it. Because he thought she was sharing it. He'd remember her contrite face and her relaxed face. Her hands clutching the bedpost. Her agile legs and tongue. He'd remember almost every second of the encounter, and even so, even years later, he'd be assailed by the certainty that the secret he'd identified in her very first burst of laughter, the secret he hadn't stopped chasing since its inaugural moment, had passed before his eyes, both transparent and voluminous, and he hadn't noticed it. A hippopotamus. He'd never be able to explain, not even to himself, not even at an age when definitive decisions are made about everything that has already happened, what that woman had meant in his life. If she had meant. If she'd been part of his life. The only thing he knew for sure, the thing he'd remember, would be the connection. Something somehow unreal but powerful. Something shapeless. Something frankly banal. A shared defeat. The presence of evil, which was frightening, then fascinating, then frightening again.

The Incredible Shrinking Woman would insult him when he got home, brandishing her index finger. She'd scale his shoulder with the quiver on her back. Bending over his right auricle, she'd remind him that he had to dress her or feed her, or at least keep her entertained.

"What does the Incredible Shrinking Woman do in the she-bird's nest?" he'd ask.

"I do what the she-bird does," she'd respond, winking. Childish and sexual at the same time. Carnivorous.

Then he'd stop thinking about the identity of the Murderess, the Detective's secret, the Professor's safety, and turn on the TV instead. But the Incredible Shrinking Woman would position herself in front of the screen. In a kind of miniature theater, akin to the Chinese shadow puppetry where silhouettes perform against a back-lit cloth screen, she'd dance with the TV characters as they advertised their merchandise. Sometimes, depending on the story-line of the commercials, she'd jump or spin. Other times she'd take off her clothes and stretch out before the rectangle of the TV set as if it were a totem, languid as a circus diva.

"You're my taboo," he'd murmur, touching the tiny creature's skin with the enormous tips of his man-fingers. Her hair. Her breasts. Her torso. Her legs.

"I'm your sister," she'd reply, already mistaken for the onscreen images, groped and uneasy. "I'm your equal."

The genetic resemblance? The twin failings? Exhaustion or loneliness? What was it that sparked this desire to touch, to touch inside?

"An expert in the subject," Valerio would mumble, half-drowsy or entirely out of it, "said a serial killer is interested, more than anything else, in probing around inside. Causing a wound. Peeling back the fold. Observing. Discovering. Implicating himself."

"Son of a bitch!" the Incredible Shrinking Woman would exclaim. "I can get inside you."

"Am I missing something?"

"I'm telling you that I need a forest."

The sound of the coin scraping the concrete city walls. That line.

Sometimes, very seldomly, he'd catch himself repeating the phrase "I do what the she-bird does." Even at an age when he'd struggle to remember things, he'd catch himself, not without astonishment, not without a certain sense of the absurd, pronouncing, singing to himself, in fact, words that only later and by dint of discipline would he associate with something else. Repeating the phrase "I do what the she-bird does" would make him think of her, the Professor. A spark. Something involuntary. He'd remember, once in a while and because of that phrase, that he'd kept her inside for days at a time, from dawn to dusk. Three hundred sixty degrees of a life. He'd remember that he'd observed her meticulously, with an apprentice's rigor: this is a woman's life. A woman isn't a she-bird. He'd remember that she ran, she ran a lot, she ran all the time. She ran even when she didn't run: breathing frenzied, gazing out into the beyond, fingers tensed. Pleasure. He'd remember that, as the hours passed, as he got used to his routine, he'd learned her face by heart and that, later—he couldn't explain it; he didn't know if there was any possible explanation—he'd erased it. In fact, there were days, entire days, when he was convinced that he could decipher her. Her gestures like letters in a book. Familiar territory. He'd remember, more than anything else, her fear. The livid pink of her lips. Her half-closed eyes. Her faltering voice. One against the other, her hands. Rubbing. He'd remember that she often struck him as smaller than she was, lesser in size, in age. Fear caused that in her, that collection of fragile expressions. That's what Valerio would remember when he remembered her: a fear he found illogical and therefore suspicious. What did a woman have to fear in the age of the Castrated Men? A she-bird. A woman isn't a she-bird.

In the testimony of the fourth castrated man's friend, the worry would become increasingly obvious. It was no longer a personal fear by then, but paranoia. A cloud of dragonflies. A pod of lobsters. Frenetic destruction. Young men would seek, and eventually find, new ways to protect their genitals, hiding or camouflaging them. Turning them, in any case, into something else. The Something Else. Old men would speak of other, always better times, now gone. Before all of this was happening. Before, when a man was safe. Before, when it was possible. Women would gradually get used to provoking disproportionate suspicion. Some would harness the new fear-induced quotas of power to transform themselves into living legends; others, most of them, would stress by all available means that they didn't harbor any castration fantasies in their minds. No one would believe them, of course, but the generalized distrust would make them double down on their efforts instead of desisting. In sum: the world, in the aftermath of Four Castrated Men, would be different as a result of being so very much, or exaggeratedly, the same world where the Detective would fail once again, this time with great pomp and circumstance, in all the headlines of the evening papers:

---

## EXTRA – *THE DETECTIVE'S MIND*

**PRICE $4.00 / No. 14421**

### BRUTAL CRIMES: MAN DISMEMBERED /

### OTHER VICTIM IS YOUNG GIRL

Photo: Two city politicians: blue ties / black suits / wedding rings / gray hair: they exchange papers across a table. A right hand: a white fist emerges from the left-hand corner of the image. In the center, right between the politicians' shoulders, the witness: steady gaze (on something within), horizontal mouth (the lack of a kiss), white shirt (smell of lemon detergent), gray hair (very gray).

[Info. p. 9]

PAGE 9: The headline or headshot or gunshot: the names of the first striking fatal resounding definitive sentences aren't without a measure of violence. The language isn't without violence. The cover. The jacket. The frontispiece. None of this isn't without violence. What's here, before your eyes, isn't without violence. Violence isn't without violence.

---

And what about the little girl?

And why should I keep my wits about me in the presence of death? Why should I pretend castration isn't also my own fear? Why shouldn't I write in my third-person singular and move like a fish along the shore of time? Why not? Signed: Your Equal.

---

## EXTRA – *THE DETECTIVE'S MIND*

**PRICE $4.00 / No. 14478**

### MACABRE! NAKED MAN IN ALLEY

### SIGNS OF TORTURE

Photo: Four paramedics around a stretcher / mobile / narrow / white sheets / mustard-yellow straps. Three men, one woman. Two with blue face masks, two without face masks. One with a helmet, three bareheaded. White gloves. Bent elbow. Ponytail. Stethoscopes against their chests, around their necks, silvery. Sheets of paper. Red crosses. Wall. Aluminum scraps. A body: motionless / horizontal / red shirt: in the middle of the photograph. His course through the world. His course through speed. A scene dominated by the crepuscular hue.

[Info. p. 9]

PAGE 9: The little girl isn't without violence. The little girl. The iris. The pupil. The eye. This open eye. This eye of yours. We aren't without violence.

---

Torture does exist. And why couldn't I also be her and be inside, very deep inside her head, watching everything from there? Why not populate / fill / substitute everyone in the summery conjugation? Who forbids me? Who will stop me? Sincerely yours: Your Equal.

---

# EXTRA – *THE DETECTIVE'S MIND*

**PRICE $4.00 / No. 14523**

## ANOTHER CASTRATED MAN

### POLICE STUMPED

Photo: Blood on the face, spattered. Blood under the body: a puddle. The body on the asphalt, face-down. The blade, mercurial. The line of a remote horizon. The rupture: bloodied, the hand. The sex. What have we done with the gifts of sex?

[Info. p. 9]

PAGE 9: What should one do when witnessing a death? Should one's face be turned to the wall? Should the weapon be hidden as the weapon that has just killed and silenced? Should one vomit onto one's own fear and then vomit again onto the fear of others? Should one shake uncontrollably? Should one mentally write a newspaper whose front page is hung with the headlines of the day, announcing each and every failure of the unconscious?

---

And what about the little girl?

Years later, walking around a lugubrious park with a woman, their hands barely interlaced, Valerio would recall how, just as he'd seen the body of the fourth castrated man, he'd remembered, and with sudden clarity, that a saxophonist lived in his building. Strictly speaking, he was a young man who studied music at a specialized institute and every evening, with a discipline that defied all fluctuations of mood and weather, he'd practice his instrument. The saxophonist, whom Valerio rarely saw on the stairs, was his Faceless Man. He'd thought of that, he'd remember years later. He'd thought about how, if his life depended on it, he absolutely would not be able to describe the face of that neighbor who practiced musical exercises upstairs. As the rhythm of the music seeped into the scene of his memory, mobilizing everything inside it, inside the scene of his memory and inside his body, Valerio could more clearly discern the silhouette of the Incredible Shrinking Woman who, as if she were a woman of human proportions, would sway along to the notes of the musical exercise. But he'd only remember this later. Many years later.

# 60

## Women and Children Die, Too

On one of the subsequent days, drinking a glass of water in the Detective's home, he'd reflect on his strange reactions to reading the messages signed with the name of a woman, of several women. He'd look through the dirty window at the world illuminated by spring light and could, at the same time, see himself reading the deceptive, semi-anonymous papers one by one. A reflective thing. The matter of glass. He'd read them so many times because the vertigo or senselessness was slow to kick in. He'd read them alone and aloud and accompanied by pencils and in the middle of his bachelor pad. He'd read them beside the Incredible Shrinking Woman, who would sometimes wipe away his sweat or distract him with her sisterly or she-bird demands. He'd read them in the bathroom, picturing a new crime, fearing it. He'd read them and cover his genitals—yet another young man, suddenly old, longing for a world that had once been better. Much better.

"Someone," he'd angrily murmur. "Someone is having fun with all this."

"And what's wrong with having fun?" the Incredible Shrinking Woman would ask with her Lilliputian ignorance. But he'd shake his head, stroke her minuscule mop of hair, gaze out the dirty window in the Detective's apartment, and take another sip of water, and none of this would excite or reassure him.

"Is it a woman who poses as a woman being a man? Or a man who's the opposite and her inverse?" the Detective would interrogate herself without looking away. From the day. From Valerio.

"Are they a monster like you and me? An aberration of the narrative?" The gibberish, just as Valerio had feared, was coming faster and faster. They were darting every which way like molecules, fearing the worst. Courting the worst. Producing the worst.

"What about the penises?" Then, unable to say more, they'd drink water as if they'd found themselves on a deserted island, under the mythical sun-warped palm tree. Nothing, no voices anywhere around them.

In later years, in his memories as an old man, Valerio would think over and over again about these delirious conversations with the kindness that only, though not always, the passage of time can create. He'd see the Detective's wide-eyed stare and once again feel the same hard, forked tenderness, the urge to shake her up from the inside. From the outside. He'd see her hands, her belly, her groin, and he'd feel, once again, the thrill of it all. The enigma of the body. Under the poplars, on the edges of lugubrious peripheral parks, slipping along, sometimes, as the young man he no longer was, he'd once again feel the violent desire to bring her with him, stuck to him, inside his pocket. A rock. A circus ticket. A key. A razor blade. He'd then hear, listening intently, the clamor of the black birds, hidden in the leaves of the trees, disturbing the sky.

"This is what you do to avoid abandonment," he'd murmur to the toes of his shoes. "You get old and hunched and you remember."

The ragged breath. The sound of blood in his temples. The wild cawing of the birds.

"You get old and hunched and you remember."

They'd talk about suspects all the time. About possible suspects. They'd try to establish a profile of the killer by meticulously investigating, as any expert in serial killers would advise, the characteristic features of the signature. A macabre rubric. A countersignature. The first name on this lethal list would be the professor's. It wasn't just that she'd been the first Informant; it was also that her occupation, her most peculiar occupation, gave rise to constant questions. What did she really do, other than spend hours in front of a screen and conduct banal conversations with basically adolescent girls? Was reading actually an occupation? How could she return to reality after spending hours sinking into worlds that didn't exist other than in the imaginings triggered by printed words on a page? Wouldn't someone like her—someone who had also read Pizarnik, and who would weep at the thought of one of her poems, as the Detective had witnessed multiple times—be the guilty one? Didn't she have, as the expert in serial killers had put it, an unhealthy interest in *looking inside*? Wouldn't that interest suffice to open the wound? And wasn't that, at the end of the day, what writing is? The questions would have multiplied infinitely if it hadn't been for the appearance of the second name that would be, in fact, several women's names, all false. The author, or alleged author, of the messages slipped under the door had desisted too quickly for them to obtain an impression of their non-textual nature, an image of their real life. But was there, the Detective would wonder more and more often, anything that could, strictly speaking, be called Real Life? They'd consider and ultimately rule out the name of the Tabloid Journalist who really was a journalist; the names of two local technicians with a somewhat morbid and incomprehensible fondness for material aspects of the morgue; the name of a window washer, an agile young man who carried around a pocket-sized book—in his pocket, no less—

while he washed the high windows of the writer's building. All, however, would have alibis, or would prove in some way or other that they hadn't been at the scene of the crime at the time in question.

They'd consider the possibility that the killer was a woman, and the explanation of the events would then be transformed into an ideological matter with eminently emotional premises: jealousy, rage, spite, impotence. They'd consider the possibility that the killer was a man, and so the castrations would become an erotic matter with wholly sexual premises: a question of possessing the masculinity of the other, wresting it away from him; a question of penetrating and tearing off. They would often even consider the possibility that the killer was both a murderer and a murderess at once: an extreme case of identification in which he or she tried to reach his or her opposite or equal, swiftly and therefore violently, due to the desire for alterity. By dint of altered desire. A writer, then? A tabloid journalist? A window washer? A pair of technicians? Who could escape that classification? Who could escape that incessant desire? Valerio, for days at a time, as he sought to protect the professor, also devoted himself to observing—with the tense calm he would remember about his activities in those days, and since he spent many hours lurking around the building—the window washer.

In his memories, the Young Man always appeared in his strange birdlike position: suspended at the height of a window, beholding impossible worlds inside. The cawing amid all that. He was risking his life, but he still scaled the heights to ensure that those enclosed within could have a clear view of the outside world. In his opinion, as he told Valerio, few people actually paid any attention to that outside world, settling instead for staring at the window of the television set.

"At least," he'd said, "I get to breathe the open air. And to look at the world from up above. If only you could hear that silence!" Valerio looked up and noticed, for the first time in a long while, the quality of the air. The smell of it.

"But you must have seen the note stuck to the window," Valerio insisted, showing him the incriminating piece of paper. "How do you expect someone who doesn't wash windows to tape it onto the outside?"

*This is my last message. Forgive me, but I get sentimental. I can't with the two of you; you're a real pain. That's why I'm stopping. Because you two won't.*

*I'm leaving the page stuck to your window, on the outside, so that when you walk in with the unimaginative woman, right when you both freeze with shock and fear, you'll think that I could be a man who cleans windows in tall buildings, or that I could be a mechanical bird, or that I'm you, Cristina, or her. The Detective.*

*Now you're pausing, right? Now you're getting closer. Now you're placing your hands on the glass (like you do, sometimes, like you do, some nights) without touching it. The message is untouchable. You just discovered it. The message is untouchable. The message is on the other side of the glass.*

*I'll leave you, then, with your suspicion.*

*(Yes, this is a laugh. This is, indeed, a cackle. Yes.)*

The Young Man pondered his response, still touching the paper. He made calculations. He exhaled discreetly.

"Given enough time, it's possible to open the window from the inside and unscrew the screens. You can lean out a little, extend your arm. Something like that." He went quiet, doubting what he'd said.

"What if there wasn't enough time?"

The Young Man pondered again. This time he gave the paper back to Valerio. He made calculations again. Exhaled.

"It's only the third floor," he murmured. "Someone agile wearing the right shoes could climb up the outer part of the building and easily reach that window."

"Someone could have asked you to place it there, couldn't they?" Valerio interrupted him, impatient to put an end to the game. His game.

"It's entirely possible, yes," he agreed, and lowered his eyes. "And much easier."

The two men regarded each other. Then, as if they'd planned it this way, they both looked up again into the sweep of the sky.

"What are you reading?" Valerio asked after a few moments, gesturing to the book peeking out of his overall pocket.

"Capote," he said immediately, in a knowing voice. *"In Cold Blood."* He stopped for a moment, then added: "Did you know it's a love story?"

A love story. The phrase would echo in his ears for a long time. His whole life, even. He'd think of it, of the phrase, years later, when he fell in love, reluctantly and belatedly, with the Woman with the Great Luminous Laughter. He'd then ponder over and over, as the weight of loneliness grew heavier than the weight of his past, whether all love stories were in fact stories committed in cold blood. That connotation. He'd eventually say yes. He'd give up. And he'd walk on with her, at her side, arm in arm, toward a shared life. *You get old and hunched and you remember.* A conversed life. A life that would produce memories.

The Incredible Shrinking Woman was the first to notice it. She said it with her usual innocence, with her typical lack of malice, with her sense of celebration intact:

"It's been a long time since a man died."

Valerio, still fearful, turned to look at her curiously. A sleeping beauty stirring.

"How long?" His voice incredulous. The echo fading.

"Days. Sunny days and sunless days."

Valerio stopped reading the apocryphal messages and removed his hand from his fly. When he stood up, it was to pour himself a glass of liquor. He was suddenly radiant. Eyes alienated and empty. Hands in the air. He picked up the phone to call the Detective, not pausing to think, and told her.

"Have you noticed yet?"

"The air is thinner," she answered. Uneasy. The voice reaching him from an abyss.

"It's been a long time since a man died," he whispered, very close to the speaker, spy, partner in crime. "Have you noticed yet?"

The silence of domestic appliances. Time. All the time. So much time.

"So what?" the Detective interrupted listlessly, bitterly. "Women and children die, too. Women and children and men are still dying, too."

Of all that time, the time he would call *the most difficult days of my life,* he would be left with the tiny dresses he'd use to garb an Incredible Shrinking Woman who was friends with a she-bird. He'd tell the Woman with the Great Luminous Laughter that they were relics of the past, fetishes. Things he'd managed to salvage after his sister's death.

"I didn't know that," she'd say, pained, longing to know more, as she touched the diminutive garments with unspeakable delicateness, with sorrowful resignation. Her fingertips suddenly magnified by disproportion. "I didn't know you had a sister."

"Yes," he'd answer with the natural absentmindedness of an old man, later, much later, as they paused under a poplar, touching its bark. "A sister. My equal. A woman with a secret."

The uproar of the black birds. The tremulous foliage. Time. The passing of time. And space. More space.

"Your sister had a secret?" He'd hear the question as if it were traveling down long dirt roads, darkened by the storm, by that laughter. He'd look at her then, searching for something that wasn't there. And he'd confirm it once more: it wasn't in any face, any face that wasn't the one he'd imagined.

"Who doesn't, my dear? Who doesn't?"

The Woman with the Great Luminous Laughter would reflect for a moment and keep walking. The slow scraping of their steps. Their breath. The waning dusk.

"A sister who loved you," she'd say later, not letting go of his arm, as if she were having another conversation entirely.

Some passerby would later say that the old couple did this often. They'd walk around the edge of the park and stop, tired, perhaps, under a tree. They'd touch it. They'd study its bark. They'd lift their age-spotted faces to look up at its broad, tranquil canopy. They'd say something to each other, he'd confess, something funny enough or impossible enough to make them laugh that way.

"Like me?" the Incredible Shrinking Woman asked when she saw him shake with rage or fear. His cheekbones acne-riddled. His eyes practically popped out of their sockets.

He touched her again with his enormous fingertips. Fingerprints like mountain ranges. He placed her in his open palm. He blew into her face: her hair in a gust. He watched her leap into the void. He went silent. Listened.

"Like you, Little One," Valerio whispered. "The ones like you are also dying. They're still dying, too."

Crick. Seldom the bones. Crack. The tightrope. Seldom all of that.

Tiny lady
dweller in the heart of a bird
goes out at daybreak to utter a syllable
NO.

# VI

---

## Grildrig

She gave me the name of Grildrig, which the family took up, and afterwards the whole kingdom. The word imports what the Latins call *nanunculus*, the Italians *humunceletino*, and the English *mannikin*.

—JONATHAN SWIFT

*The urge to shrink myself down, sit in my hand,*
*and shower myself with kisses.*

—ALEJANDRA PIZARNIK

---

# 61

# I Can Take Off My Pants, If You Like

In the basement. On a round metal stool. The man waiting for her is there: in the basement, in the harsh artificial light of the office, seated on the round stool that spins in circles. A corner. The Detective doesn't recognize him right away, but she doesn't need to ask his name. Eyes: inhabited, dark, close together, intensely curious. Hair: short, salt-and-pepper, unique. Beard: trimmed, thick, masculine. Hands: pianistic.

"I need your help." The voice: water in a well. Something deep. Something stomachy. Dark.

"Haven't you read the papers lately?" She turns her back to him. "I'm what you might call a disaster. The real McCoy."

A certain way of squinting his eyes.

"Last night," he falters. Then stops. Extends his arm: rolls up his sleeve. "Last night, on the street."

The Detective comes closer. She looks at his arm, and then, as if in disbelief, she touches it. His skin: weightless. Blue veins. Dense hair. The man unbuttons his shirt. Exposing his shoulder, he tries to show her his back.

"Is there more?" she whispers. Teeth biting her lower lip.

"I can take off my pants, if you like."

The Detective drops into her chair, brings her hands together at her chin, index fingers meeting, other fingers intertwined. She thinks, or prays. She looks at him. The-Man-He-Sometimes-Was is thinner than she imagined. There, on the stool that goes up or down at will, he also looks younger. Practically a teenager. A teenager with gray hair and a tie. Leather shoes. Corduroy suit.

"Domestic violence?" she asks. An oblique smile. Expedited indifference. "You should choose your lovers more wisely."

"Last night," he persists, not looking at her, unwittingly sidestepping her jab. "In the street. I didn't recognize him. It was very fast. The alcohol. The blow to the head."

Just then: the hum of electricity: the harried steps on the other side of the white wall: the heartbeat.

"This isn't my case anymore," she murmurs after a moment. "I don't think I can help you."

The man, motionless. His eyes undaunted. His neck. A Modigliani.

"I think you're the only person who can help me," he tells her, serene. A strange firmness in his voice.

The Detective keeps observing him in her way: head bowed, gaze toward the crown of his head.

"And why would you think something like that?"

"Newspapers never tell the truth." The smile: distant, barely there, monalisaly.

"You've got the wrong office," she says.

"Or maybe you do," he replies, seeing himself out.

# 62

---

# The Ice on the Other Side of the Window

"You won't be able to live with this, will you?" She hears the question and nods her head yes, repeatedly, without turning around to see who asked it. The ice on the other side of the window. The light from the streetlamps. The fog of her breath.

"That's not the worst part," she finally answers aloud. Clearing her throat a bit.

"What is?"

"The worst," she hears herself say, "is that I won't be able to die with this. You know?"

The Tiny Lady she's conversing with and doesn't believe in says yes, she does know. The Detective smiles, turns her back to the window, and runs her fingers through her hair.

"Don't you think it's time for bed?" she murmurs with exaggerated sweetness. The reek of rum in her voice.

"Don't treat me like a little girl," she hears her say. "Because I'm not."

"All right," the Detective replies, at peace. Her eyes back to the window.

*Hekinah degul. Tolgo phonic. Borach mivola. Quinbus flestrin.*

# 63

So Why Did You Think of That?

He wondered it often. The-Man-He-Sometimes-Was never stopped wondering. When the Detective who had overseen the case of the Castrated Men appeared before him uninvited, without an appointment even, out of sheer coincidence (or so she said), he expressed himself as quickly and frankly as he could. He confirmed that he had indeed suspected her.

"But that was a long time ago," he also said, in a tone that sounded more like a belated apology. "I'm not sure I'm remembering things clearly."

The Detective had then ordered him, with considerable tact, with a somehow feminine geniality, to remember.

"It's important," she urged.

"For whom?"

"For the dead," the short-nailed woman said, looking at him. "Who else?"

The-Man-He-Sometimes-Was mulled this over for a long time. He glanced at his beer, his wristwatch, the other men in the bar. The racket distracted him. The images on the TV screen. He took another swig. He licked his fleshy, eager, denotative lips.

"It might be important for you, too. For your career," she said at last. "You can't deny it."

The Detective looked at herself: the paltry scraps, the fragments, the physical weakness. Her mental weakness. Her indiscipline. Her world. A world of uncontrolled impulses. A bottomless world, a shapeless one. A bottom she was always sinking into: temptation. Her head cracked open on the blue tiles of an empty pool. What shouldn't happen: a stack of bones, flimsy as chopsticks. A breakable thing. A mental thing.

"That's over and done with," she mumbled, and didn't add anything else. She didn't explain whether she meant the case or her career or herself. Her eyes on nothing in particular. Her fingers drumming on the tabletop. The din of the place. The images on TV. The men. The other men.

"I understand," whispered the man with short, gleaming, salt-and-pepper hair. The voice like water in a well. Something fresh and deep, from somewhere else. Something stomachy.

She said she wanted to start from the beginning, and he replied that there was no beginning. That his story had no beginning. That any story that warranted being called a story was nothing but the continuation of another: its erasure or postponement. The Detective thought those must be someone else's words and asked him, once again, to recall the motive. The initial motive. He responded that there were no motives. Not for that. Then he listed all the ones he could possibly imagine. Finally, he said he'd been with the Suspect because they both believed in it: in the impossibility. The impossibility of being together.

"Were you?" The stress on the verb tense.

"Yes," he answered, as if it were obvious, or as if he didn't understand her question.

"That's when everything started happening, is that right?" the Detective said abruptly. "Right then."

"The murders. The messages." His brow furrowed as if the connection hadn't previously occurred to him. "Around that time, yes. I always thought, actually, that our sudden closeness had to do with all that, more than anything else."

"With the murders?"

"With all of it," he said wearily. "With the other man who'd just passed. With the smell of death. With the terror of living that way, always on the verge of losing everything."

"Was that when you learned she was the primary suspect in the case?"

The-Man-He-Sometimes-Was let out a burst of laughter. He glanced back at the TV screen and, paying no attention to the rapid-fire images, pulled a pack of cigarettes from his jacket pocket. He took one out, not looking, not looking at her, either, and lit it in the same way, preoccupied, lost in thought. He took a hungry drag and almost instantly blew out the smoke with a greedy sound. Fleshy, his lips. Grooved.

"She found it funny that I thought about it like that." He winked. "I wasn't the only one, either."

"And what made you think of that?" the Detective interrupted again. "It isn't the most romantic idea in the world," she said in a quieter and quieter voice, regretting what she was saying as she said it, going back to observing what was all around her.

They'd been meeting at the bar where the Detective had run into him just weeks before. They'd sit right across from each other, at a circular table, right before customers came in for happy hour. Young men. Students. The unemployed. That kind of commotion. The-Man-He-Sometimes-Was and the Detective preferred the midafternoon silence. A vacant lot. The truce of lunchtime; the chatter lingering after a meal. Then she'd switch on a small tape recorder. Then he'd start speaking. And then, often, she'd be sorry. She'd look away, turn her face toward the bar, the screen, the others.

"I don't know what made me think of it. But it was the first thing I thought," he said. "I thought she'd be capable of it. That she must be telling me as a way to figure out if I knew what she was capable of."

"But you must have had some kind of motive," the Detective pressed.

"Definitely."

"Suspecting a woman you have an intimate relationship with?"

"Suspecting?" he asked, after taking another slow, ample, leisurely pull on his cigarette. "I had no doubt. I was sure. I always was."

"Why didn't you report her?"

His hands: long, fine, bony, soft, amber-colored, pianistic. His beard: thick, trimmed, masculine. His sigh: emphatic, obvious, sexual. Dark tobacco smoke suspended over it all.

"Because what I'm telling you, my dear Detective, is a matter of fiction," he said in a quieter and quieter voice. His eyes inhabited, close together, curious. "It was, after all, a love story."

"There are four castrated men in this case."

"More," he said, forcing her to remember. Reminding her that he did remember her failure. The failure of the Department of Homicide Investigation.

"More, yes. There are more than four real bodies in all this. Many more," she acknowledged. Then she looked down and reached for her beer. She drank. Stayed silent.


There's a man and a woman at a circular table. The only illumination in the scene is the beam of a powerful spotlight shining directly onto the beer foam. *Prey to the question: Who is killing me? Whom am I giving myself to kill?* There's a man. A table. A beam.

"I'm not going to ask you for help," she says at last, haltingly. "I wish you would help me. That someone would help me. That someone would care. But I'm not going to ask."

Ears: open, alert, a net with a pair of dead butterflies inside.

"So it's true you never found any evidence," he murmurs. "Such a brutal case and no evidence. No motive. No weapon. No penis. Nothing. That's what your investigation led to. Nothing."

"You're the man who knows too much, don't you think?" the Detective whispers. A glass of beer between them. Head down. Gaze up. The-Man-He-Sometimes-Was right in the middle, in her sights.

"That's what I was asking for back then, do you remember?" he asks later, much later. "In your office."

"What?"

"Help. I was asking you for help."

"Of course, yes. Help. But I won't beg for it."

"Why would I do something like that?"

"What?"

"Help you, of course."

"I don't know," she also answers much later, avoiding his eyes. "I don't know why you'd do something like that. Out of fear, maybe. Or revenge. Because you were about to die. I just don't know."

There's a woman and a man at a circular table. Outside, the rain turns to sleet. The winter drags on.

They'd fought on the night of the attack, it's true. The motive could have been anything. A bad mood. Fatigue. A glass of water. Jealousy. He'd gone out (and he still remembered the sound of the door as it slammed: sonorous, coffin-y, final). He was in search of alcohol, of course. Alcohol and noise. He was in search of someplace where he wouldn't be identified as half of a unit. A one of two. A mythical better half. He asked this of the taxi driver: to take him to a trendy, expensive, anonymous place. When he parted the red curtains and stepped into a stuffy, foul-smelling room, he knew it wouldn't be expensive, but it was certainly underground. It would do just fine. The warped music. The volume. The scent of sex and cigarettes. He sat at the bar and looked up when the woman's feet appeared before him. She spread her legs slightly and used a long-nailed finger to peel back the cloth concealing her vulva. The-Man-He-Sometimes-Was leaned closer. A damp nook, he imagined. A site of particular softness. Supple. The woman turned around. Bent over, head between her knees, her hair a waterfall, she showed him her anus. A small pursed mouth. An unpainted mouth. He slipped a bill under her platform shoe. On his feet now, he thrust his hand into the woman's body. The warmth. The wetness. What he'd imagined. He wanted to be deeper inside. He wanted to be completely inside. To supplant her. To be the hand protected from the cold beneath the cloth of the glove. To be her. Occlude her. Be the woman's secret body. See through her eyes. Feel what she was feeling. Open. Inhabited.

He was slow to emerge. When he did, he felt like he was returning from a long journey, or like he was being born. Something broken-down or rearranged inside him. Something radically new. He parted the red curtains for the second time, now in the opposite direction, and once he was back outside, on the street, with the night wind in his face, with the scarf coiled around his neck, he heard the footsteps. Pounding. The vast echo growing and growing in the empty night, inside his head. He wanted it to be her, the woman. He heard the echoing footfall and desired, with an overwhelming desire, for it to still be her. The supplanted woman. He was about to turn around when he was enveloped in darkness. A gloved hand over his eyes (a blindfold). The grappling. The hand struggling for his zipper. Not a word, meanwhile. Not a shout. Just him and terror. Just him and terror and the grappling of bodies. The sudden certainty of the end. He remembered the photos in the newspaper. What was left afterward: the remains, the fragments, the miserable ruins of a body. The butchery of its entrails. A finger here. A phallus there, somewhere else. The unknown place. A terrible cruelty: the clash of two or more wills. That strange poetry drenched in blood and eyes. He wanted to run but couldn't. He needed to urinate. His knees buckled. He wanted to fall. That was the last thing he desired before he entered an even greater darkness: to fall. An atrocious desire to yield. And then, in the end, though he didn't know how, the awakening. The pain in his bones. His eye against the pavement.

The first thing he saw when he finally lifted his lids was her face. The face of the First Suspect. Her hand was resting on his forehead and she was looking at him tenderly. He struggled to associate this gesture with her, the woman he'd tussled with for some insignificant reason the night before. Her white teeth distressed him. All white around her. All silence. The hospital room.

"You were lucky," she whispered in his right ear, keeping her hand on his brow. The smell of toothpaste. The pressure of her fingers. The sense of being at the edge of a cliff, overlooking a chasm. The air all around. He didn't know which of them said *this time*.

There's a man and a woman at a circular table. The rain has stopped outside. The sleet. The winter through the window.

"I'm scared," he confesses. "Really scared."

The Detective observes him, her expression unchanging. That gesture.

"Of course you are," she says.

# 64

## *Relplum Scalcath*

"I don't want to have this discussion with you again," she heard. "I don't want you to ask me again."

"You got it, Grildrig," said the Detective without a trace of irritation. "I won't. Why don't you just eat. Let's just eat."

The sound of soup slurped into the mouth. The smell of cooked vegetables: that softness. The warmth of the space. A tiny table on top of the table. A toy chair. A plastic plate setting. Two women.

"I need a forest," she heard her say. "A fishbowl."

She inhaled the fragrance of pines after rainfall. Not thinking about it, she stepped onto the dark paths. Eucalyptus. Poplars. Oyamel. Her feet in the mud. Her cold shoes. The clouds. The landscape seduced her.

"Why would you need something like that? A forest? A fishbowl?"

"To rest, naturally," came the crystal clear reply.

*After much debate, they concluded unanimously that I was only* relplum scalcath, *which is interpreted literally* lusus naturæ; *a determination exactly agreeable to the modern philosophy of Europe, whose professors, disdaining the old evasion of occult cases, whereby the followers of Aristotle endeavored in vain to disguise their ignorance, have invented this wonderful solution of all diffi-culties, to the unspeakable advancement of human knowledge.*

"Of course," the Detective murmured. "Or maybe you think fear is a creature hungry for your future," she added. She noted the silence she received in return. Then she kept eating.

# 65

## The Witness

She sat on a park bench under the dry boughs of a poplar. From there, just as the Tabloid Journalist had said, just as she'd read in the messages from the Traveler with an Emptied Glass, she had a clear view of the Professor's bedroom window. It was easy to picture her behind the curtain: her hand on the pane at night. A statue. She wondered if the Professor still lived there, but she didn't know if she wanted to find out just yet. Your problem, she remembered she'd said, is no talent whatsoever. In any case, she didn't stand up. She didn't knock on her door. She just slipped her gloved hands into her coat pockets and stayed there, motionless, taking in her surroundings: joggers, baby carriages, dogs. The cold mud. The fierce wind. The leaves. After a little while, her scarf spooled around her neck, she made her way back to her basement, head bowed. Coin scraping along the wall: a line. Footsteps. Inside, under the artificial light, she made a few scribbles in a notebook. And then, sitting at the computer, she threw herself into filling out forms on the trafficking of narcotics in the northern part of the city.

She did this several more times, never altering her routine. She'd go to the park, sit perfectly still on the proper bench, and observe everything. Sometimes she'd open a brown paper bag and take out a sandwich, a carrot, an apple. She'd eat slowly, her mind elsewhere. She'd meticulously chew each bite. She'd swallow without relish. Then she'd get to her feet, wind the scarf around her neck, and walk away.

If someone had asked her what she was looking for, she wouldn't have been able to answer right away. If someone had noticed her, if her presence had piqued the curiosity of some assiduous park-goer, they surely would have hesitated. Mouth agape, a fruitless attempt to say something. A whimper. A scarecrow against the wind. The sense of usurping a place. She would have kept silent, if someone had berated her, and then, with the sudden courage of the truly shy, she only could have told the truth: that she didn't know what she was doing there. She had no idea what she was looking for.

She understood it later, though, with total certainty. On the (unusually sunny) afternoon when she saw the Man-He-Sometimes-Was enter the First Suspect's apartment (swift steps, head held high, a gleam in his eyes), she knew why she'd spent so many hours on that bench, under the dry boughs of the poplar. So she hadn't been there; she'd been with her. Present indicative. If someone had asked, she certainly would have said, "I'm a witness to a love story. I'm a voyeur. Don't you get it?" Then she would have laughed at herself.

# 66

# A Jar of Formaldehyde
# A Jar of Jam
# A Sample

The news shook her. Sheer electricity up her spine, then a strange heat all over her body. Her thighs. Her forearms. Her fingers. She stopped at the kitchen counter with a bite of sandwich in her mouth and stared at the screen. She didn't chew. She couldn't take her eyes from it. She couldn't shut her ears. There, in the small luminous rectangle, the Detective saw it. The Detective saw the jar. The jar that the Traveler with the Emptied Glass had mentioned. Inside: a penis. Inside. The Detective was about to call Valerio, To Say: Valerio, but she managed to react in time. A young man, with long arms and stained teeth, was narrating the sequence of events that had led him to find the glass jar on top of a boulder in a vacant lot.

"The boulder was right by a willow," he murmured with a tremulous, fascinated voice, glancing compulsively at the contents of the jar he held in his right hand. "A willow," he repeated. His eyes toward the camera, exuberant. The need to communicate something, to make himself understood, to stay onscreen. When she switched off the TV, the Detective could see the rhythmic swaying of the long dry boughs. A melancholy scene. The boulder. The jar had been carefully set down at the base.

"So you do want me to find you after all?" she asked the air. The moment of swallowing.

She'd wondered so many times: if the penis isn't on the body, where is it? The question overwhelmed her. If it wasn't in the street, a waylaid appendix. Flesh of my flesh. If it didn't turn up. If it kept disappearing. She'd walk and wonder incessantly. Under what? Inside what? Years of this. Nausea, sometimes. Besides electricity, she couldn't say what else was coursing through her skeleton. She was frozen in place, but she could feel the brusque, haphazard careening of her molecules. The flowing of her blood: a torrent. The murky beating of her heart. The peculiar feeling of having received a personal message: it flooded her. The feeling of being a fool. A sudden breathlessness. The feeling of reading too far between the lines of an evil book. Overinterpretation. The feeling of witnessing the elegant, unusual move of the inveterate gambler who had all the cards in their hands and tossed one onto the table just so they wouldn't end up alone, bereft of a game, an opponent. Someone was having fun with all this. Someone hadn't stopped having fun with all this. The answer overwhelmed her: the penis was in a glass jar, beside a boulder, under a willow. Intact.

A jar of formaldehyde. A jar of jam. A sample.

The memory flashed into her mind as an unbroken image: a row of glass jars in a museum display. There were children, lots of them. Noise. They filed in two by two, holding hands, a natural science class, biology, chemistry. Something basic. The monumental door. The narrow halls. The voices suddenly hushed, whispering. That's where she'd seen them for the first time, perfectly arrayed on a wooden shelf. There they were: the glass jars. Outside: labels with names. Inside: indecipherable creatures. The smell of stored objects. The reek of formaldehyde. She'd approached with extreme caution.

"Do you know what it is?" her teacher had asked, a man with a necktie, a gelled cut, and nose hair. A grown man.

"No," she'd answered sheepishly. Her hands clasped behind her back. A fledgling scientist.

"It's a fetus," a foul-smelling mouth informed her, so close to her ear that she feared it might bite. "A deformed fetus," it repeated. Rotten teeth. Cave-breath.

"This is an ear," she heard. The index finger on the transparent surface. She turned around to look at him. The Grown Man studied the contents of the jar with a peculiar fascination.

"This is a six-fingered hand," he continued.

"But what are they doing here?" she dared ask, stunned.

"What do you think?"

She repeated the question to herself: what did she really think? But she couldn't come up with an answer. She didn't think anything. She couldn't believe it, actually. She couldn't believe what she was looking at. The Grown Man's face. The collection of jars on the shelves. A biology class. Something basic.

A jar of formaldehyde. A jar of jam. A sample.

And what could be more deserving of preservation than desire? the Traveler with the Emptied Glass had asked. This she remembered. This she confirmed in the copies of the messages she desperately searched for on her jumbled bookshelves. The tiny handwriting: a line of ants. The ink like wine and bones. Message No. 5. The consistency of the stolen object; they'd written that, too. Someone doesn't have a penis. Someone wants a penis. The famous case of envy? *Do you think it means something, Cristina?* A man who's searching for something he lost? A woman who wants something she never had? Just then, she was overcome with an urge to tell her off, to show her once and for all what she was capable of. She, who wasn't.

A jar of formaldehyde. A jar of jam. A sample. She grabbed her coat and rushed off to the Museum of Natural History.

# 67

## Childhood Is the Key

I say I'm here, the Detective thinks. She places her hands on the steering wheel. Presses on the gas. Her face the image of her face a reflection of her face in the windshield. I say this is the rain the rain falls falling comes naturally to the rain. She drives. The red seeping through the wet glass is a diluted red. A monstrous red. I say the jar is real and the Traveler with the Emptied Glass is also real and the knife. She advances. In bumper-to-bumper traffic, she advances. That's what it feels like. She respects the traffic lights. The color red. I say I'm alone in this. This is a tunnel the eye of the needle a pair of shoes a heartbeat. Something that trembles inside: pulse, sex, breath. I say they write. Someone writes messages. This is a message: I'm alone in this. I drive. Speed. She thinks this. I say the imaginary as impossible, the ruled-out as useless, is real. The fear is real: the fear isn't real. Fear is. I want to be read: that's the message. The penis is the key. I say none of this is inside me. I drive. I'm a drove, driving. I'm moving through the city, she thinks. She thinks about the willow. Valerio. To Say: Valerio. The willow boughs swaying with the wind in the wind. A waltz. She needs something a different something a wound adrenaline. The penis, it's the key. I say that seeing her face is a unique proposition, she thinks. My face in the windshield, she says. She sees it. I see it. I say everything is real. She advances. A willow. The honking seeping through. A squeal. Metal on stone. A saw. I say that everything seems to be right in front of me it's right in front of me it seems, she thinks. A hand emerging from the dark wants to be seen doesn't want to be seen wants to trap the dark. I say I'm the dark. The desire to kill, she feels it. Homicidal urges, she feels them. She thinks that she's the dark. It's not so crazy to want to kill to be able to not be able to kill. The heat in the hand in the finger the fingertips. Rage: a red color beyond the windshield. A badly wounded red. The penis is the key. The message is the formaldehyde. It's natural for rain to fall the rain falls the. Matter of waiting. Someone is having fun with all this. Someone wants to play to write to read. Someone wants to be read. I say I'm illiterate, she thinks. Devoted readers, she repeats. *If you keep reading me so closely I'll stop writing, devoted readers, is what I'm saying.* She's saying all of this. She presses the gas the chest the laughter. To die laughing. Hands on the wheel. Her forehead. Illiterate, she says.

When she peers into the glass jars still lingering on the shelves of the Museum of Natural History, Grildrig, swimming: Grildrig clinging to a yellow-tailed fish, pressing her palms against the glass; Grildrig releasing oxygen bubbles through her open mouth, saying:

"So why did you believe that childhood was the key?"

The Detective is in a hurry she hurries around the shelves. This is called breathing. Then she stops. She does it without thinking without feeling without hesitating. The walls of the room, she realizes just then, are green.

"This is a penis," the Grown Man murmurs, very close to her ear. The cave-scent: something before time. The hunched stance of a secret or humiliation.

"And what is it doing here?" she asks. Her slight pink open

mouth very close to the enormous nose. Can an echo be a melody? I say I'm here, the Detective thinks. She repeats it. Her fingertip on the surface of the display case that protects reveals conceals the jars. My face in the glass, she murmurs, beholding herself. I say I'm alone in this. When she counts the jars on the shelf, one two three four, she turns around and looks at the guard. Breathes.

"How long have you been working here?" she asks him on her way out. His glasses (tortoiseshell frames), his belly (ample), his mannerisms (parsimonious). The man stares at her, motionless. When he finally motions to the small hearing aid in his right ear, the Detective asks again.

"So many years I can't even remember," he immediately exclaims. Buoyant.

I say that everything seems to be right in front of me it's right in front of me it seems, she thinks. A hand emerging from the dark wants to be seen doesn't want to be seen wants to trap the dark. I say I'm alone in this.

# 68

## It Could Have Been You

Gelatin-silver. Twelve by twenty centimeters. Black-and-white. The face. The body. The castration. Twelve images. A selection. Something cruel. An aesthetic.

"The black you see here," she tells him, pointing at a spot within the frame, "is blood."

The-Man-He-Sometimes-Was says nothing, a glass of wine in his right hand. Mothball perfume. As if it needed clarifying.

"It could have been you," the Detective murmurs, already regretting it. "But," she adds.

He looks at the photographs. He picks up the first by its upper right corner, studies it, and slips it behind the last. Again. Another. Again. Man with a deck of cards. A poker game: no expression.

"Who took them? The coroner?" he asks. His eyes: inhabited, close together, intensely curious.

"I did," the Detective says quietly, suddenly ashamed.

The Man-He-Sometimes-Was smiles. More a burst than a flash of lips. More an extravagant luminosity than a warm light. Then, dark socks on the floorboards, he slips along, approaching. A cat or something larger: a leopard. The soft ripping of his steps. The taut silence.

"You're not a professional," he says, "but you could be. Did you know that?" The sound of the second hand somewhere in the house. The sound of blood quickening in the body. The sound of the car when it revs up and fades away. The smell of burnt rubber. All here. All now.

"I'm not a child," she states with remarkable slowness, looking him straight in the eye. "Make no mistake about that."

"Everyone knows you're not a child," he says in the same deep, calm, youthful voice. "You never were," he adds, winking at her, his left eye. "Everyone knows that."

More an illumination than a warm light, his smile. More a sock than a leopard, his approach. The floorboards. His house. More a closed door than a back, his silence. More a slap.

"It could have been you," she says, repeating herself, saying it to him. The air that changes places. Another car, somewhere else. She looks at him intently. She remembers, now, as the vehicle moves away, that he'd appeared when death did. *Only death hurls us so furiously toward the unfamiliar body.* That the Man-He-Sometimes-Was replaced another with a Luminous Laugh. She tries to remember. She returns. *Why not ask who the hell is speaking.* The desire to ask about him, now. About the other. The desire to ask about the other one, the abandoned man. Can a man be the lone woman in the desert and the threatening traveler and the little metal girl? Was Alejandra Pizarnik a man? The victim or the murderer: what could you have been?

"Would you like me to identify something?" he asks, picking up the photographs of the castrated men again, stepping away.

She studies him as if through a great cloud of dust. A dune. Another country.

"Something, yes," the Detective murmurs. "Something I don't know."

She observes, uninhibited, the bulge between his legs. She notes its faint stiffening. Its way of growing.

"I understand."

"You're the one who's been closest," she says, lowering her eyes. I say I'm illiterate, she thinks. "You're the only one who's escaped all this alive."

"I understand."

The subtle tick of the second hand. The ripping steps.

# 69

## Fine Restraints

*I lay down on the grass, which was very short and soft, where I slept sounder than ever I remembered to have done in my life, and, as I reckoned, about nine hours; for, when I awaked, it was just day-light. I attempted to rise, but is not able to stir; for as I happened to lie on my back, I found my arms and legs were strongly fastened on each side to the ground; and my hair, which was long and thick, tied down in the same manner. I likewise felt several slender ligatures across my body, from my arm-pits to my thighs. I could only look upwards; the sun began to grow hot, and the light offended my eyes.*

*I heard a confused noise about me; but in the posture I lay, could see nothing except the sky. In a little time I felt something alive moving on my left leg, which advancing gently forward over my breast, came almost up to my chin; when, bending my eyes downwards as much as I could, I perceived it to be a human creature. . . .*

Grildrig climbs. The bow cuts across her body; the arrows are gathered in a quiver at her back. She sweats. The effort required to scale a shoulder. Its roundness. Its softness. Then a shortcut: the ear. The cheekbone. Grildrig tugs at an eyelid with both hands. Success: she sees the eye. The unmoving brown iris. A very light brown. A nearly yellow brown. An autumnal forest in there, inside the iris inside the eye. The leaves, dry. Melancholy, the swaying and shifting that scatters leaves onto the leaf-strewn ground. The lips, barely a scar on the face. Grildrig inserts a hand. Then a foot. The damp. The tip of the tongue that. She changes her mind; hoisting herself up to the chin, she slides down the neck. The sternum. The ford of the belly. The fleeciness. A body, she thinks looks touches savors. This is a body. She presses on. Then she stops. Here, she thinks declares signals. Here is the wound. The cut, precise. The blood. The guts. The innards. Grildrig sits at the edge of the wound, legs dangling eyes peering in. Curiosity. Temptation. The urge to. She jumps. Grildrig jumps. Grildrig is inside.

A woman is inside a man. An incredible shrinking woman sniffs roots observes. A woman observes: there's a woman inside a man. There are fine restraints all over his body, the man's body. The man who lies, immobile, would only, if he could, see the sky.

Grildrig forges her way inside the man. She sweats, or she's slicked with the viscousness. The effort of walking around the interior. She shouts for shouting's sake to hear her own echo. Gelatinous, the matter. The darkness. The cold. This is a stomach, she declares. This is a knot of veins. A pancreas, this. Nominal, Grildrig assails. Flesh of my flesh, she declares.

When she emerges, her arms raised, that gleam in her eyes, when the face streaked with blood spit tears, Grildrig. The Detective has observed it all. The Detective picks her up with her right hand and places her in the palm of her left.

"You need a forest," she whispers. Even so, Grildrig covers her ears. "You need to rest."

Grildrig doesn't listen to her. Grildrig, over and over, passes her tongue over her lips coated in viscous matter. More a summer evening than a ray of light, her sigh. More the pleasure.

The gleam in her eyes. The filth of her clothes.

# 70

## Accept This Love I Ask For

The idea of failure. A woman in a blue uniform lives breathes sleeps with failure. I am the failure; that's what the game is called. Debacle, a fresh receptacle. Despicable. The Detective strikes the white wall of her office. Fist. Foot. Fist. Fist. Another man. She's informed, before it's printed in the papers, that another man.

"Where?" she asks. "Where exactly?

"In the same area."

"Same signature?"

"This time they tied him up."

"The poem I mean," she interrupts. "What's the poem?"

"Accept this face of mine, mute and betting," he reads aloud, taking long pauses, taking his time from breath to breath. "Accept this love I ask for. Accept the part of me that is you," he finishes, crestfallen. The quavering voice.

The field of action. The poems. I say I'm illiterate, she thinks. Devoted readers, how do you read? What is it you read?

"An embroidered handkerchief in his right hand." She listens to the description. "Orange blossom perfume."

"Threads in the handkerchief," the Detective murmurs. "Threads in the body."

They look at each other: eyes like keys. That gleam. Desire, approaching.

"Do you really think he keeps the penises in a refrigerator?" She hears the question crystal clear.

"Who?"

"Him, the murderer."

"Or her, the murderess. Right?" she asks. She winks. Then turns around. Then says to herself: "In a refrigerator or in a museum, it's all the same."

Then.

When he leaves, when his back his neck his thighs pass through the glass and metal door, the Detective can't help but note it's the first time in a long while that she's spoken with Valerio, To Say: Valerio. The echo of his voice.

*Accept this face of mine, mute and begging. Accept this love I ask for. Accept the part of me that is you.*

When he's gone, when his absence is only an aroma, the Detective remembers that he was the one who'd once mentioned the existence of an incredibly small creature. A woman. Child's play.

And then she sees something she'd never seen before: a Man with a Luminous Laugh. That glow.

# 71

## The Adjective That Cuts

Hands: trembling, whiter than the leaves that fall and scatter, dry.
Voice: low, hollow, oscillating.
Gaze: wary, electric light, loose end, manta ray.
Lips: grooved, pale, a rose I've only seen in dreams.
Question: Have you heard?
Answer: Yes.

Pause: a slammed door, a slap, an empty parenthesis, the breath when, a way of not being there.

Scene: two bodies against a window, the poplars, a winter.
Characters: a man, a woman, suspicion, fear, sex.
Throat: dry.

Title: *a love story.*

Declaration: you scare me.

Goya's words: the worst is to beg.

Images: lip on lip, tongue, hand against hand thigh, the breath when, hair below, brushing against, the verb to grind, saliva.

Repetition: only death hurls us so furiously toward the unfamiliar body.

Coda: a man a woman sometimes.

# 72

## This Is What People Do Alone in Their Lives

Grildrig tells the Detective in a very soft voice: *He blew my hairs aside to take a better view of my face. He called his hinds about him, and asked them, as I afterwards learned, whether they had ever seen in the fields any little creature that resembled me.*

*They said no, of course. And they kept staring at me as if I were a monster or a marvel or a little bit of both. They asked me questions, or at least I assume they did, because they addressed me and released horrific sounds I couldn't decipher.*

*I answered as loud as I could in several languages, and he often laid his ear within two yards of me: but all was in vain, for we were wholly unintelligible to each other.*

"So you couldn't understand each other," the Detective sighs, interrupting the story, still horizontal on the bed. The ceiling, suddenly high, whiter than.

"That's right," the creature says with slight nods of her head. "Not even a little." Her tiny index fingers almost pressing together.

"And you think I'm going to believe you?" murmurs the woman of human dimensions as she slowly sits up, breathing heavily. The ceiling suddenly very low. A jail.

"Well, you're going to have to, because otherwise you won't be able to understand why I did what I did."

"And what did you do?" she asks.

"You know," she says, winking. "You know all about it."

The Detective freezes. Without warning, she lifts Grildrig by the back of her shirt. Her diminutive legs dangle in the air.

"You don't know what you're talking about," she says, very close to the tiny face: a gust of air in her miniature mane. "You don't have the slightest idea what you're talking about," she repeats, annoyed, before she tosses her onto the pillow. Nearly imperceptible contact. A couple feathers in the air.

"You'll be sorry" is the threat she hears with utter clarity. And it's then, not until then, that she leaps out of the bed and begins to pace around her apartment, tension and anxiety consuming her from within.

# 73

# If It Had Happened

Many years later, so many, in fact, that it felt like a different life altogether, when Valerio had resigned himself to walking slowly, his breath forever labored, he'd remember the day with absolute clarity. He'd murmur: it was a terrible day. Even more terrible than the murders. The Woman with the Great Luminous Smile would let him tell a story that she was no longer in any shape to really listen to. Perhaps that's why Valerio ventured to tell her that, on the day the chief of the Department of Homicide Investigation appeared onscreen to deliver the news, he'd done nothing but think about the Detective. As if the news justified his thinking of her, as if the act would otherwise be unthinkable. He knew about the public announcement; he knew it was so important that they didn't leave the press conference to the detective who'd headed the case. He knew the man in the dark suit and small eyeglasses would be there, on the television screens in every household, to announce the news. Valerio would recall the hours that passed from when he received word to the moment the uninspiring face of a middle-aged man declared that the horror was over. The hours, those glacial hours, had been, and this he remembered perfectly, suffused with absolute sadness. They're the hours of the most absolute defeat, he'd say. No one could convince him to attend the press conference, stationed to one side of the thronging journalists. And it was humanly impossible to draw him away from the image on TV. He wanted to verify everything. He wanted to be certain that what was happening, what he knew would happen now, moment by moment, was the stuff of his nightmares. When the face appeared onscreen, solemn with the gravity of the case, Valerio thought that the Detective, at that very instant, must be in her kitchen, eating a sandwich, flipping through a book. The image of the oblivious woman, the woman who didn't know what was taking place not far from home, in the same city, hurt him inside. Her solitude. Her ignorance.

There's a man onscreen, and then, almost immediately, there are two men. The first man gestures to the second, describing him. He says: this is the murderer. There's silence. A pause. Then a commercial break.

As soon as I saw the face of the man in the suit who said, in a deep, unhurried voice, "The murderer of the castrated men has now been identified and apprehended," I thought of them all. I imagined the sudden unease of the Detective, frozen in place, open-mouthed, her eyes fixed on the long arms, the stained teeth of the man who, just a few days before, had held a glass jar in his right hand on a similar screen. I imagined her incredulity, the way she shifted her tongue inside her mouth to produce a faint click. Her voice, saying: what people do to not. I imagined the relief of the Man-He-Was, a long sigh. I imagined him remembering, as so many others would do, that the man, that man, the second man, had pronounced the word "willow" many times, on the same screen, his voice charged with fascination. I imagined the smile of a traveler holding an emptied glass in her right hand. I imagined the Journalist, reflecting. I imagined myself, staring at the screen, unable to take my eyes from the screen, my fingers covering an open, paralyzed mouth. Then I had no choice but to accept what was happening.

There's noise, lots of it. Noise of microphones and people. The second man appears behind bars, blank-faced. The first man explains that the second man has confessed. A psychologist is already in the process of exploring his mind, he says. Then a commercial break.

The idea of failure. The skeleton. The pulse of failure. A woman in a blue uniform lives sleeps breathes failure. I say I'm illiterate, she thinks. When the Detective saw the news on her TV screen, she couldn't suppress a faint smile: more a fork cleaved to the back of her hand than an exhalation. More funeral than poplar. What people do to not.

Valerio would say, many years later and to a woman who struggled to hear, that that day, just after the news, that day he'd slumped into an armchair, his hands a bowl beneath his face, rage seizing his entire body. That day, he'd been about to get up, to dash outside and run over to the apartment, her apartment. He'd been about to knock on her door and say straight out, point-blank, his breath as ragged as it would become many years later, in his old age, I'm here to help you. Let's continue the investigation. I have time. I have all the time in the world. Let's keep going until we find the guy who did it.

"Or the woman who did it," she'd have said, with the same smile, taunting and enigmatic, winking at him. Her left eye.

If it had happened, Valerio would say much later that, without a doubt, she would have said exactly that: or the woman who did it. He'd never give up, he didn't know how he'd go about it or why, but he knew he'd never, ever give up. He bet his left hand on it, his eye, his sex.

There's a man onscreen. The man's eyes gleam, riotous. The eyes staring straight into the camera, into the center of the camera, in fact, are the eyes of a realized man. The pupils: open, impish. Someone, no doubt about it, is still enjoying all this, somewhere else.

# 74

## Watching Her Sleep

She rests. Now she rests. Just a body, something negligibly small. When she wakes, when she recovers the dimensions of wakefulness, Grildrig. But now she rests. A cocoon at most. Something soft, pliable, between the legs.

The Man with the Luminous Laugh watches her, fascinated.

A glimmer.

Another.

# VII

## Death Takes Me

*Anne-Marie Bianco*

# 75

# The Epigraph

*A book—for me, made by me—the journey of the consciousness through a state.*

—CARIDAD ATENCIO, tr. MARGARET RANDALL

# 76

## The Crossed-Out Title

Years later she would write, for me, since I'm the one who's asking, this: ~~A LITTLE BOOK OF BROKEN LINES~~.

---

# 77

## Certain Luxuries

Almost a year ago, in November 2005, I received a package—
under peculiar circumstances, as the package was sent to the address where I'd lived only until the age of thirteen—containing
the manuscript of *Death Takes Me*. It was accompanied by a brief
note in which the author asked me to consider her book for publi-
cation in the poetry series of the press I run. Of course, we don't
usually receive these sorts of requests, or at least not in this way;
Bonobos is still a small independent press, and our catalog is partial to poetry with practically no exchange value at all in the publishing market. But the note was hardly the smallest of the enigmas
that fell into my lap (these days who among us has the patience
and capacity to seek out an old tenant, a stranger!, and send them
a package?). The greatest mystery, or the most obvious, was the
author's name: Anne-Marie Bianco. At that moment, I couldn't
recall any poet of that name—local, regional, or even continental.
But her last name sounded familiar. Days later, prompted by a
situation that had nothing to do with this one, I suddenly remembered the name of an Italian author (Italian or of Italian descent)
who, in the sixties and seventies, had published a handful of poems
in literary magazines here: Bruno Bianco. Thanks to [*crossed out*],
with whom I discussed the strange package incident, I remem-

bered two more things. First, there was a time when some people suspected that Bruno Bianco was the pseudonym adopted by a well-known group of poets who met with some frequency in a popular cantina in the [*illegible*] neighborhood [*handwritten over the text:* full of very tall buildings and houses with stained glass windows]: the now-mythical [*crossed out*] Bar. And second, that the construction of those scattered poems was—if I had to define it in just two words—broken and unsettling. What's more, [*crossed out*] and I recalled that Bruno Bianco's poems were marked by an odd sense of intangibility, which we attributed to the themes chosen by this peculiar poet and how he addressed them. In the end, we agreed that these characteristics made Bianco's presence in our national literature a memorable one, however brief. Bruno Bianco: a poet's name that contains, in its two constituent words, an irreconcilable contradiction: Bruno (dark) Bianco (white). Bruno Bianco: an eccentric character who perhaps never existed (at least physically). Bruno Bianco: the abstract poet. Bruno Bianco: poet as sign. Under this influence, I reread *Death Takes Me* and, as you might suspect, decided to publish it. I was reviewing the galleys when I received a second note from Anne-Marie Bianco. Perhaps predictably at this point, it arrived at another residence I hadn't lived in for many years. This time she wanted to know the editorial verdict. She also included an address and a date for a future meeting. On the day in question, half an hour before we'd arranged to meet, I made my way to the high-ceilinged, stained-glassed hotel where I was supposed to finally make the poet's acquaintance. I sat in the lobby and looked around. I didn't even know whether I was waiting for a young woman, an old woman, or a middle-aged man. Suddenly everything seemed to fit inside the name, inside Anne-Marie Bianco: the slender frame of a made-up male poet's daughter; the silhouette of a woman, now aged, who decides to shatter the pretense of masculinity and show herself; the diagram of the man she always was or will be. My blunder became overwhelmingly obvious. There I was, the head of a tiny regional press, awaiting a ghost in the lobby of a hotel milling with people who, like me, seemed lost, searching for something. Of course, Anne-Marie Bianco didn't show up for our meeting. Or maybe she did, but wanted to avoid detection. In any case, that day, which was the appointed day and the appointed time, I didn't meet Anne-Marie Bianco. I never learned her motives or what she'd read, apart from her obsessive explorations of Alejandra Pizarnik. I never learned her age, her birthplace. I never saw her fall silent or smile. But a small independent press can indulge in certain luxuries. This one, for example: publishing a faceless author in a world where the face has become a kind of dictatorship. Or this one: investing in a text, a text alone, for the text's own sake and nothing else. The book you hold in your hands, then, exists in place of that meeting. It's the faceless text that begins with the calm of a question, a riddle. You, the reader, if you so choose, can decide whether you want to construct that face and implicate yourself, if necessary, in that enigma.

MATÍAS R. DE HOYOS, editor
Bonobos Press

# 78

---

## This Wound

## (Which Is a Wounded Word)

I

### THE SCENE OF THE CRIME

You ask me for a story. I [*crossed out*]
a return: to the blood (that blood): you ask for my notes.

A story: It caused shock and horror. A discovery. The lifeless body of
a man. The depths of an alley. Blindfolded eyes. Bound feet, bound
hands.

A means of adjectivization: Brutal homicide. Ill-fated citizen. Tragic
case. Dreadful surprise.

A means of narration: . . . wrists tied with tape, arms pinned above
his head . . .

The scene of the crime.
(What is a scene? What is a crime?)
A ditch. An alley. A darkness. An abandoned house. A skeleton.
A garbage can. A coffin. An apartment on that corner. A corner.
A park. A moan. A tunnel. A broad daylight. A street. A fast lane.
A faster lane. Faster.

This wound (which is a wounded word): a crime.
This way of shattering and falling: a scene.

[*crossed out*]
Another lifeless body. Another citizen. Signs of mutilation.
(a way of uttering.)

What is the news?

This dying in the public eye, this
a way of saying *my death that takes me*
*in the throes of sex, it's true*
emblematically
a certain scent of groped paper
exclamation point, punctuation mark, extra
sign
an excess. Yes. That.
A newspaper.
Dying in the eyes' excess: dying in front of you,
open.
Dying in the languid writing of the words to die, hopelessly.

You ask me for my notes. You ask me for my eyes rolled back. You
ask me (on behalf of what?) to take a step and then another and
uncover myself, as open as the news, dismembered like your dead,
before the mirror of your page. Your desire.

You ask me for so much. You do.

A way of stopping short to think: The early inquiries. The victim.
Preliminary versions. All pending confirmation.

# 79

## Front Page

(EVENING EDITION)

II

MACABRE!

This morning
a man (approximately thirty years of
age): was
found dead
bound at the feet and hands and eyes (blindfolded)
in a ditch.

(That's how I wrote it.)

The police are already
(investigating the case).

# 80

# Early Inquiries

III

## THE BODY AND THE LINE

Those were the days of metal desks, of green screens, of instant soups. The days of all those deaths, they were. I remember them. I remember them well. I remember everything. My red dress. My hunger (I was always hungry). My relish for the sudden cutting of a phrase.

We never talked about Pizarnik, you and I.

We never talked about her prose. Her troubles with prose. Her desire for prose. Her (unsatisfied) desire for prose.

As men died (because it's the fate of men to die) marked by the
sharpened object, I'd cut the phrase. With relish
I'd open the line (like a can of sardines)
the probability of another. I'd split
one hand to the right and the other to the left
the body in the middle, the body

marked by the opening of the line
would fall. Bled out.
The body alone.

The Tabloids would declare it the following day: we never
talked about prose.
We should talk about prose. Prose is [*illegible*].
To be discussed.

# 81

# The Tabloid Journalist and Death: A List

## IV

### TO GO AND NOT RETURN

To go to the Public Prosecutor's Office and return from the Public
Prosecutor's Office. To go to the death.
To ask questions about the death.
To photograph the death. To fall silent
before the images of the death. To be cold.
To write about the death. About the questions surrounding the
death.
To write: death. To separate the syllables. Unravel letters.
*To write* death. To open it.

(A can of sardines. A tombstone. A window.)

To never return from death.

To remain in death.

# 82

## Secondary Inquiries

V

### THOSE WHO VERSIFY DON'T VERIFY

Who verifies the line (something that stabs) (something that enters) in the heart of the knocker?
Who versifies the door and, below the door, the light seeping through?

I'm gifting you the line begging lethal unfinished.

Put the seeped light into the door of your body (the mouth in other words) (the nasal orifice) (the sexual orifice) (the crack).

The line enters and breaks on entry. The line is the weapon: [*illegible*]

A line of coke.
A line of light: a sword. That dusk. A horizon.
A line of words (broken latches).

A line of periods (and semicolons). A line of doors ajar.
The line of your lack. The line of your slacks.
The telephone line (dying).
The line that splits you in two.

Who versifies? Who versifies the versifier?
Who verifies?

I am the witness.

---

# 83

# Who the Hell Is Speaking?

VI

*VICTIM* IS ALWAYS FEMININE

In the Public Prosecutor's Office (which is a scene of the crime) (a scene of crinum) (of climes).
In the body (which is public) (which is open) (which is a corpse).
In the cut (within the cut) (under the cut, for fuck's sake) (at the very root of it).

Who's speaking there? Who is the first person of our singular?
Where do I weep?

In the silencing crinum: verdigris green, place.
Revengemerald.
In what's open (which is the scene of the crime).
At the very root of the cut (which is public) (which is a Prosecutor's Office).
In the body. Within the cut. At the very root of it.

And why not say sparely, strictly, simply, that the corpse lies face-up
on the narrow autopsy table?

Why not say that it's February and [*crossed out*] cold?

In the clime (which is a body) (strictly).
Before the corpse (which is a victim) (which is feminine) (which is
grammatically).
Before the public (which is language) (these lines) (latches).

At the root of it: Why not ask who the hell is speaking?

Sparely.

# 84

# The Tabloid Journalist and Death:
# Another List

## VII

### IT'S TRUE, DEATH TAKES ME

In your sex
(armorplate bladecut crossingout) (keyslot)
in the here of everything in the world, death
(which is this parenthesis) (and this one) takes me

I smell I eat I look I grieve: a verb collection

the she-bird of desire in the nest: a portent
it's true, death is true
and takes me, munificent little missile in mourning, in the
plural sex.

First person. Speak, for fuck's sake, first person.
My mouth.
My tear.
My zipper.
My need.

My notes. You want
my notes

Do Re Mi Do Re Mi Fa Sol Sol.

It's truly death. My grief. My shotgun.
My suspicion. My guilt.

Foreground: the body face-down. Arms bound above the head. The
bandaged face. The pants: around the knees.

I see I burn I watch I hush I grieve: second verb collection.

Nothing will ever be the same.

---

# 85

# The Female Imagination

## VIII

### THE MALE IMAGINATION

There's a vast esplanade. And above the unexplained esplanade in all its vastness, there are gusts. Gusts of air and dust. Afghan gust. A veritable gale. Then the body appears. Alone and singular, right here. A green veil over it, the body. A dagger under it, the veil. The perpetrator: the desire to cut. The time it takes for the desire to ripen: the blade. The process of sharpening. The rasp of the sharpener. A master plan.

The music of the object that slims the object. Stone on steel. In certain places, that's called *screech*. Molars clenched. Skin prickling. In certain places, that's called being cold.

The game is called *I am*. Who walks across the esplanade beneath the gale? Under the veil: a she or he. Over the veil, with rage: the gust. Something is walking right across the page that has no explanation.

A murderer or murderess. The desire to wear glasses. The game is called right here. It's called enraged, the esplanade.

There's a dwarf on a tabletop. A tightrope. A many-metered distance: abyss beneath. There are two arms, outstretched, that make a puzzling equilibrium. There's a mouth. Beneath it all there's a mouth. The mouth says: the game is called *I am*. The mouth goes out at dawn and speaks the syllable. It says: No.

The tabletop can be an esplanade or else a page. Music of steel on skin: an around-it-all. That screech.

An esplanade that's an immaculate hand. To brandish is a synonym of to wield, an antonym of to let go. The hand brandishes the weapon and lets go of the rest. The glow. Furrows in copper plates. Furrows in plates of skin. A vengeance, this. This is.

A very tiny woman knows.

---

# 86

# The Suspicion

IX

INSIDE YOU INSIDE ME

The eye approaches the door (the latch).

To shirk to howl to cloud to leave behind: my third verb collection.

Someone inside you sharpened the blade inside me
(the audible music is made by insects)
someone inside me raised the shout inside you
(the glimpsable space is the longest hunger)
someone inside you played the instrument inside me
(a guillotine and its echo) (a button) (the space between the brows)
someone inside me cut the butterfly inside you
(the boulder on the precipice).

The eye shuts (serrated animal) and the insect in the space of the
longest hunger falls with the vertical weight of a blade of grass. The
guillotine falters.
Someone inside you cut that blade inside me
(illness sighs)

someone inside me opened the latch inside me
(a long cry)
(the music of the machine)
(a sleepwalker).

Inside me someone inside you slits wrests harms excises mutilates
(a fourth verb collection).

All we need is a forest. A fog.

The eye opens inside you (a door inside me).
The latch clicks.

---

# 87

# Autopsy

( A L O V E   S T O R Y )

X

## THE VISIBLE SCENES

*In situ:* a space, a bedroom, a rectangle, a page.
The body in the middle.
A metal bed. A hose. A pail.

A fictional character: the corpse.
A fictional character: the mortician.
(A love story.)

The instruments: a saw, a knife, a hammer.
(Tools of the trade.)

The action: upward, the skin of the face. A mask. *Death's business is to strip.* The saw against the skull: the noise, the smell of smoke and brains. Upward, the knife inside the belly. The hammer on the sternum. Crick. Crack.

(This isn't a narrative poem.)

The writer: a coroner who writes down everything that emerges from inside.

The reader: the public prosecutor who accounts for the events.

(A love story.)

The smell of blood in all of it.

# 88

## The Smell of Blood

XI

MINUSCULE DESCRIPTIVE [*ILLEGIBLE*]

It's as if you'd vomited for a long time and then vomited some more (a sunrise, along a wall marked by the narrowest side of the coin. That line). What's left on the crushed teeth, behind the lips once closed, in the mouth's human dampness. The appositive phrases "bitter but sharp," "rotten but ethereal," "sour but red."

---

# 89

# I'm Afraid of Winter

# Afraid It Will Go Away

XII

A CONFESSION

The gale. That came to pass.
The news. The photos in the news. The mothers' tears.
Time (this is a narration) happened.

The blade passed over the body. Oh so cinematically!

*Close-up:* the open pore, the hair-root, the wrinkle-crease. The
grime.

*Close-up:* the staring eye. The blood that's just been flowing

the blade of grass (the metal of the guillotine) over the bird's
commotion
the animal I am. A hypnosis.

*I'm afraid of winter. Afraid it will go away.*

That happened: the cloudy day.
The Great Seer declared war on Herself.
And lost her body.
And lost the dawn (and Dawn [*crossed out*] is a woman's name).
She lost her hand, centrifugal. The stars withdrawn.
The fingernails.

(An army of the dead dances on the head of an angel with a pin on his plexus.)

She lost the future (time-thing, slipping).

I saw all that in the news.

And who made the plant, the beast, the victor?
It could be cold (and that too came to pass).

I'm really a journalist.

# 90

## Dimensions

XIII

ENLARGEMENT EFFECT

The Enormous Woman sinks her shoe
into the grass. Her eye
a circle like a halo around the sky. Her hand
a tombstone that covers the insects' path. Astral
the wails. The guilts. The I-regrets.

Contrition.

All this to say Saturn. To Say: It never rains.

The sharpest light.
A hand surrounds the bedroom where something will happen.
The door, opening.

Did someone ask about the direction that the line of ants would
take?
Did someone halt the parade where the dead dressed up as the dead?
Did someone weep, dumbfounded?

*Those towers are the place for dealing with what continuously postpones its arrival.* Someone always said the bit about the two colossal legs, the tall straight grasses, the fabled minarets.

Below: the plain.
Below something would be about to happen and wouldn't happen and wouldn't stop happening.
The cooing of a docile pigeon.

The door, closing.
The silent moccasins of the one who's leaving.

The Woman of Taste, [*crossed out*], [*crossed out*], the
Beyond.
(Someone would say that about the way she fell. About her way.)
The one imagined in the camera of the dusky ailment. The More
Than Seen.
(Someone always said that about a personal film.)
[*crossed out*] The barefoot one who slips along the tremendous
thimble of Herself.
The Enormous Woman who vomits and then vomits
some more

(that smell of so much blood, of more).

Below: the knee against the pavement.
That trembling. The plain like grief. The broken knuckles. The
scalpels.

All to write *what I write holds a vigil for the corpse of who I never
was.*

So why not fall? And why not fall with all my weight? Why not fall resoundingly into the hollow?

The Enormous Woman enters the bedroom of The Gaze. The sharpest light.

The wail.

# 91

---

## Copyist

XIV

DEEDS AGAINST THE DEAD

You ask me for my notes. Do Re Mi Fa. Do Sol. My stave. My
memory.
You'll be sorry, I told you.
A tree sick with birds. A sad animal.


The worst is to beg.


I didn't understand why you would
be sorry or for what. And so I'll run even faster
without looking back, guided


the invisible hand on my chest


(that universe)
(once and again, once and again, again and yet again).

Out there: *Great Deeds Against the Dead*. In there, Goya.

A copy in time. An incessant replica.
A pretense.
Oh! Malice. To beg (which is the worst).
To give.

# 92

## Credits

XV

### THE ORIGINS OF THE PERFORMING ARTS

In his essay "Aeschylus, the Lost," Ismail Kadare writes in Ani Kokobo's translation that mourners were "the first incarnation of the ancient choir." They are entrusted with expressing a pain that isn't theirs on behalf of everyone else. To mourn doesn't mean to cry. The mourner is a pretender. The mourner is an actor. The mourner asks for notes (Do Re Mi Fa Do Sol) because the worst is to beg. To obtain. [*crossed out*].

# 93

## You'll Be Sorry

XIV

A BOOK FOR ME

The echo and the echo's hand: an answer that isn't.
The echo's origin. A balm,
this way of being at peace: something solved.


Everything in its right place.


So what is a place, what is a crime?


It's saddened by the fern. The loam. A crime.


I'm writing a book for me. I read
aloud what writes me and what strips me
(death's business is to strip).


The sentence cuts the page in two. The tongue. The body.
You'll be sorry, it says. The book

I write for me reads me aloud
(death's business is to interpret).

There's a bouquet of arms and legs. Brains.
All on the table that's a coffin that's a door.

Something opens from inside. Look.

I could have given you a key. I could have delivered you peace.

# VIII

Don't Tell Anyone We're Here

# 94

## The Crushing Process

I received *Death Takes Me* in the mail. I hadn't requested it, as she seems to suggest in certain passages of her texts. I never asked for her notes. I never wanted them. I simply received the little book in a standard manila envelope through the university mail service. And I opened it as I open so many useless mailings: without enthusiasm or curiosity. It was midwinter by then, a new semester. A foreign world. It's no exaggeration to say that I felt like vomiting once I'd read it. Fear or anxiety. Anticipation or verdict. Anne-Marie Bianco. I glanced around my silent office as if someone were about to knock on the door. Everything indeed seemed about to. An enormous hand at a tiny door. And me, there, even tinier. And you, asking: is the city a cemetery? I balked. I took a deep breath. I went to the windows: the world outside carried on beneath a delicate coating of ice. The gray sky. The sky, then, abruptly blue. A thin, sharp blue. The city is a cemetery, yes. It wasn't until I returned to my desk that I picked up the envelope again and looked, without realizing the futility of my intent, for the sender's information. Nothing there: no name, no address, no scribble. There was the blue stamp traversed by lines of black ink. There were the characteristic scratches of travel. There was my name as the recipient. But there was nothing at all about the Tabloid Journalist who was, without a doubt, the author of the text. Anne-Marie Bianco. I barely remembered her: that's how ordinary she was. But as soon as I read that book, that tiny book, I knew it was her. I was still afraid as I dialed the Detective's phone number, but rage was brewing, too. *You'll be sorry.* The threat. The jeer. Her interpretation of me. Her memory of all that. Her way of reading and butchering me in one fell swoop. Her deceitful analysis. *Why not ask who the hell is speaking?* Her appropriation of the facts. Her collection of verbs. Her betrayal. When I told the Detective I had something that might interest her, it took her a long time to react. You watched me, meanwhile, empathetic. Eyes full of a certain shock; something, in any case, intimate. I sensed that the Detective was struggling to even associate my name with a specific person, a face. I sensed that she didn't remember yours, either: your face. In the end, as if her response were caused by chance or fatigue, we arranged to meet at the restaurant on the other side of the Alley of the Castrated Men. The smell of old blood. The sound of some distant commotion. The hazy memory of the bodies. The sheen that. The Detective arrived on time. Her nails short. Her gaze opaque. Her accent strange, almost imperceptible. I gave her the book right away, barely stopping to greet her. The blue uniform.

"And you think this might interest me?" she asked before she opened it. Then she read it in front of me, racing through it, as was her way.

The crushing process. The flow of the game. The extract.

"So you never spoke with her?" she asked, incredulous, angry, as soon as she looked up from the text. "You never spoke with her about Alejandra Pizarnik?"

"No." The confirmation like a latch forever shut. Sawed off. "Never."

*"Death Takes Me,"* the Detective repeated in a very soft voice, very slowly, as if trying to remember something important. "A book. A little book, right? A book made of broken lines."

"As if she wanted to incriminate herself," I said. "Or exonerate herself. Or exonerate someone else."

The Detective smiled and lowered her gaze. Something had changed in her, but I couldn't quite place what it was.

"There's more and more of it," she added, cuttingly. "But truth remains very difficult to prove."

It was time. The way time traveled through her voice. It was part of the change I could sense but not identify in her.

"Who publishes this sort of thing?" she asked, returning to the topic of the book, still deep in thought.

"It's a small independent press," I said, pointing to the name. "That's the editor's name," I added. My fingertip suddenly enlarged by the typeface.

The crushing process. The trickle of acid. The potion.

"Some would call this poetry, wouldn't they?" She looked me up and down, as she did when she was pondering something. "A collection of broken lines. A collection of illegible things, crossed-out things, brackets."

Somehow I managed to say yes and no at the same time. I took a sip of water. I looked her in the eye, imploring.

"She hasn't forgotten anything," I murmured. "She's still living in that time. She could do it again."

We were silent for a long time. We looked up at the ceiling. We looked out the windows: a beggar peering in, hands framing his face, gazing through them. We looked toward the pitcher of liquid. The liquid that shook like a leaf.

"Describe her again, please," she asked. She'd already picked up a pen and napkin when she said, "She always looked like a sketch to me, the study for something that might eventually become a woman." It was obvious that she remembered her. "A tense cartoon. The blueprints of a house about to be built, or about to collapse."

I interrupted her. What I said as if in a trance was: "Shy. Apprehensive. She'd constantly repeat the word 'really,' as if she feared she wouldn't be persuasive otherwise, as if she had to be. That's it. Persuasive. Straight hair. Split ends," I continued. "A certain hunch to her back. A whole world there, on her shoulders. Willful. Unable to take no for an answer. Stubborn. It's impossible that her name was *actually* Anne-Marie Bianco. Hands cracked from working—" I stopped then. Stopped short. I looked at her. "Hands cracked from working a job that wasn't, by all appearances, being a journalist."

"Dammit," the Detective muttered, dialing another number. "Valerio," she whispered into the receiver, "remember the case of the Castrated Men?"

The crushing process. The trickling bile. The toxin.

# 95

## An Area Closed Off by a Circle

"But what's an incredible shrinking woman doing inside a nest?"

That's what a he or a she would say. Or more than just one he or she. Or one containing many. A they.

"She's doing what the she-bird does." This would be a wink.

The Incredible Shrinking Woman would leap from the palm of a hand and land in the center of a circle. Eyes like flashlights. A stage. A place called Brobdingnag.

"Don't tell anyone we're here." A quiet voice.

"Shh." A vertical finger against two pink lips.

"Can you keep a secret?" The head nodding up and down, down and up.

Time would pass like this. And you'd pass over, then, to one side of time.

The stage would exist, naturally. The open eyes would exist, fixed in a circle, illuminating the middle of the stage, producing it. The Incredible Shrinking Woman would exist, no doubt, because the shining flashlights of her open eyes would exist, and so her shadow and her bones would exist.

Because she would exist, because her existence would be in-controvertible, she could ask: "Aren't you going to tell me any-thing today?" in a genuinely exasperated voice. Arms crossed over her chest. Brow truly furrowed. Tapping her right foot and then her left.

"No, not today," she'd hear. "Come back tomorrow." A hesita-tion. "Later. Come back after tomorrow. And then after that."

"And you," she'd add, turning to look at me right at the end. "We're not on a first-name basis, got it?"

All this in the enormous palm of a hand (which is a world) along whose lines the dead walk slip stumble (three verbs only).

A book. This is a book. Someone once said that everything would take place in the winter of a book. I'm afraid of the book. Afraid it will go away. The winter. A climate's language. The cold. Someone would narrate: The woman returned many times, sometimes to ask and sometimes just to prove she could. It was just a useless, repetitive action. A lurking.

# 96

Prey to the Question: Who Is Killing *Me?*

*Whom* Am I Giving Myself to Kill?

The headlines of the evening papers put it like this: TERROR RE-TURNS: BRUTAL ALLEY ATTACK.

*castration allows the subject to take others as an Other instead of as the same*

Valerio, many years later, would say that after closing the still-unsolved case of the Castrated Men, when the Department of Homicide Investigation had already disbanded their team and assigned each of them to new investigations, they received a strange book. He'd recall the moment: the phone call, the seconds it took to recognize the voice, and then the matter at hand. His exhaustion. His incredulity. His urge to hang up. He'd agree that, in this moment, he didn't want to hear anything else about it. The case had been too complicated, too emotional, too dark. Someone had gotten away with something. Someone had had fun with all this. Someone or multiple someones had dragged him into depths of himself that he had no desire to visit ever again. He didn't want to experience failure ever again. Most of all, he didn't want to talk to the Detective ever again. He'd say, later, that he was on the verge of hanging up, that he was already searching for a more or less polite way to do so, when she began to read certain sections of the text aloud.

"The peace of something solved?" he would have stammered. "That's what it says? I could have given you peace? That's how it ends?"

The Detective's laughter would have made him hesitate. The dirt path. The storm. The sudden smell of water. For a moment, he'd remember much later, facing himself in his bathroom mirror, his drooping cheeks white with shaving cream, he would have felt able to return. Eager to return. He would have remembered the countless days with no answers. Overwhelming, the days. A whole world there, on his shoulders. The helplessness. The rage. The unease. All of that suddenly eclipsed by the light of the word peace. Its letters' peaceful glare. For a moment, there, his lips at the receiver, damp, anxious, he was convinced that they could continue investigating the brutal homicides, even without the approval of his superiors, until they solved them. Between one case of petty drug dealing and the next, between one instance of organized car theft and the next, they could continue meeting outside of working hours, he thought in that instant, to read poetry and ask questions until they stopped making sense and proved strange things. They could ask: "Do you need a forest?" And then answer each other: "The idea is the excitement of thinking." Amid the routine that already dizzied him with boredom, amid all the everyday things, and there were so many of them, they could keep reading—he was about to believe this—texts between the lines and look all the way into each other's eyes.

"Yes, Valerio, that's what it says," the Detective would then interrupt euphorically, unusually optimistic. "Exactly that."

"Have you already talked to the person who published the book?" he'd remember asking her, animated, still eager to participate.

"Yes, but nothing came of it," she would have said, the Detective, still unhesitating, still certain that the end, the long-anticipated end, was approaching, hurtling closer with clumsy zeal. "All he knows is what he says in the prologue. That's it."

"He never met her?"

"No." The swift response. "As if she doesn't exist in real life."

"Anne-Marie Bianco." He would remember how he repeated the name very close to the receiver: an invocation, a mantra, a prayer. "A strange name, isn't it? A false name, don't you think?"

"A bodiless name," she'd answer, attentive, cautious. "Or a name with the wrong body, in any case. One that would seem to be a woman's, but who knows."

"A name that's lots of hidden names. A name that doesn't yet want to be associated with anything concrete," he'd whisper after a moment. "You know what that means, don't you?"

Many years later, and even after many years later, almost at the end of time, he'd remember perfectly what he did next: He closed his eyes. He rubbed his closed eyes with the fingers of his right hand. The distance between his head and feet suddenly vast, concrete. A sad giant: that's what he was. The air thinning out between his lips. His exhalation both slow and thunderous. His eyes open. His feet. The chime of bells from somewhere. Seven.

"It means, Valerio, that the name, the other name, the hidden name, the original, if you will, doesn't want to be uttered," she would have said, with painful pauses after every letter. "That's what it means. That she doesn't want us to find her."

Valerio would have remembered her voice just then. Her other voice. The voice with which she'd given up. Before, years ago. The voice that had informed him of the obvious: that children and women and men were still dying. They would keep dying. The voice with which she confirmed a fact. An unaccented voice.

"I know," she'd have added. "I know it for sure. But is that how you read poetry, Valerio?" There was water in her question, lots of water, old buildings, shoes, sweeping skies. Memories.

"We never figured it out." He would remember his response, the way he expressed it: unexpectedly solemn, with a firmness he wouldn't recognize as his own. "That's not how you read any of this."

He would tell me years later, more and more slowly and in a fainter and fainter tone, that she had undoubtedly understood it faster, faster even than he had. Just as a woman does. He would acknowledge that the Detective hadn't insisted. The silence. Her silence. He would remember that forever. He would say that he could hear her breathing through the receiver. Her steady breath. The cawing of many birds.

"You're right, Valerio," she'd said then, at the end. "That's not how you read poetry. Not like that."

"And that was it?" I asked when I realized he was stopping in the shade of a tree, his breath a panic of birds, fearing the story was over. "That's not how you read poetry. That's it?"

Valerio said nothing. Avoiding my eyes, as if I were no longer there, he devoted himself to touching the bark of the tree with absolute care. His fingertips. His pink nails. The dark blotches on his skin. The inclination of his body, his mind. When I interrupted his loving inspection with the same question, that was it?, the old man turned to look at me. He drew his lips taut. He looked at me.

"At the end I asked if she still believed it was possible," he whispered.

"What?"

"That," he said in a very low voice. "That someone, that a murderer or murderess could give her peace. I asked if she wanted that. Peace."

*that leaves death in the second person*

The Incredible Shrinking Woman would say, with the tempered tone of a happy foreigner, with her celebratory innocence, that someone, without a doubt, continued to have fun with all this. She'd look skyward and confirm, with a great sigh, that it was still winter.

*inscribing some sign on the surface of a dismembered body*

"I'll remember this moment," I said in the soft voice of fright or intimacy. "I'll remember it in the future."

The Detective had just said: that's not how you read poetry. Not like that. Then she'd turned off her tiny phone.

Murmurs. Food being swallowed. Forks against knives. Water glasses. Footsteps.

I tried not to see her, but I saw her. I couldn't close my eyes. I don't want to, no. The expressionless face. The face stripped of face. An esplanade. A space for walking toward. I grieved for her. She passed by, then. This. She turned to look at me.

"Strange things happened that winter," she murmured, her lips barely parting as she spoke. "There were other winters, many more, actually, when other strange things happened, but the ones that winter were—" She cut herself off. "There will be others. I suppose."

She shook her head. Time. All the time. She touched the little book of broken lines and rested, cautiously, like someone trying to prevent harm, her gaze on the cover. She wasn't a beautiful woman, I thought. She lifted a glass of water to her mouth. She lowered her eyes.

"Anne-Marie Bianco," she said softly. Then looked up. I don't know why I felt protected rather than exposed by her gaze. "Will the answer always be a fake name?"

We both smiled.

"The worst is to beg," she blurted. "She's right about that."

"Today isn't September 25, 1972," I said in a quiet voice, not looking away from her. She smiled again, reluctantly. Then I closed my eyes to see something else, to see something more.

*"Why not say who the hell is speaking?" she asked.*

*"Nothing," she asserted, "it will."*

*"What's the purpose of a cup?" she added.*

_____

# 97

# You Have No Right to Know
# Anything About the Dead

The victim's body is covered up.

This is a veil.

Beneath the veil, the dagger.
Above the veil, the gust.

The gust is your breath.

We violate a book in order to read it, but we offer it closed.

—EDMOND JABÈS

*Toluca, State of Mexico, April 5, 2003.*
*Prague, Czech Republic, April 27, 2007.*
*Mexico City, Mexico, Durham, North Carolina, and Houston, Texas, 2021.*

# Sources

Translations of Alejandra Pizarnik come from the following sources: *Diana's Tree*, translated by Yvette Siegert; *Extracting the Stone of Madness: Poems 1962–1972*, translated by Yvette Siegert; *A Musical Hell*, translated by Yvette Siegert; "The Lady Buccaneer of Pernambuco or Hilda the Polygraph," translated by Suzanne Jill Levine; and *Selected Poems*, translated by Cecilia Rossi. Other, previously untranslated translations of Pizarnik's work—from *Poesía completa, Diarios, Los perturbados entre lilas,* and *Alejandra Pizarnik: Prosa completa*—were made by Sarah Booker and Robin Myers for this novel.

"Clouds Within / Clouds Out There" by Caridad Atencio, translated by Margaret Randall, published in *The Oval Portrait: Contemporary Cuban Women Writers and Artists,* edited by Soleida Ríos.

ABOUT THE AUTHOR

CRISTINA RIVERA GARZA is the award-winning author of *The Taiga Syndrome* and *The Iliac Crest,* among many other books. Her latest book, *Liliana's Invincible Summer,* won the 2024 Pulitzer Award for Memoir and Autobiography, and was a finalist for the National Book Award. A recipient of the MacArthur Fellowship and the Sor Juana Inés de la Cruz Prize, Rivera Garza is the M. D. Anderson Distinguished Professor in Hispanic Studies and director of the PhD program in creative writing in Spanish at the University of Houston.

## ABOUT THE TRANSLATORS

SARAH BOOKER is a teacher and literary translator. Her translations include novels by Mónica Ojeda and Gabriela Ponce as well as other works by Cristina Rivera Garza. She is also an associate editor at *Southwest Review*.

ROBIN MYERS is a poet and translator. Her translations include books by Andrés Neuman, Claudia Peña Claros, Isabel Zapata, and Cristina Rivera Garza.

ABOUT THE TYPE

This book was set in Caledonia, a typeface designed in 1939 by W. A. Dwiggins (1880–1956) for the Merganthaler Linotype Company. Its name is the ancient Roman term for Scotland, because the face was intended to have a Scottish-Roman flavor. Caledonia is considered to be a well-proportioned, businesslike face with little contrast between its thick and thin lines.